SUD

Clay Allison casually spat in Collier's face. Collier's features clouded with rage, and Jessie saw his hand move shakily toward his weapon.

"Go on," Allison urged. "Do it, mister."

Collier hesitated, made a fist, and dropped it to his side.

"Well, shit." Allison looked disappointed. Without warning he reached under his coat and drew his revolver, thumbed back the hammer, and fired it directly in Nat Collier's face. A sharp explosion brightened the night. Collier's features vanished. The side of his skull blew away, splattering the canvas wall, and he slumped limply to the floor.

Allison jammed his revolver back in his belt. When he turned, his eyes darted through the crowd and found Jessie. "Let's go," he said softly. "I think Miss Mattie wants to talk to you, girl."

Jessie shrank back in horror. . . .

➤ WESLEY ELLIS ➤

LONE STAR

AND THE
SAN ANTONIO RAID

A JOVE BOOK

LONE STAR AND THE SAN ANTONIO RAID

A Jove Book/published by arrangement with
the author

PRINTING HISTORY
Jove edition/December 1983

All rights reserved.
Copyright © 1983 by Jove Publications, Inc.
This book may not be reproduced in whole or in part,
by mimeograph or any other means, without permission.
For information address: The Berkley Publishing Group,
200 Madison Avenue, New York, N.Y. 10016.

ISBN: 0-515-07353-9

Jove books are published by The Berkley Publishing Group,
200 Madison Avenue, New York, N.Y. 10016. The words
"A JOVE BOOK" and the "J" with sunburst are trademarks
belonging to Jove Publications, Inc.

PRINTED IN THE UNITED STATES OF AMERICA

Chapter 1

Sand and dry grass tugged at her boots as Jessie made her way back from the beach to the shelter of the dune. Collier had made a fire, and the heavy aroma of coffee smelled good. Dropping an armload of driftwood to the ground, Jessie brushed her hands clean and stretched. The motion hollowed her belly and tightened the cotton shirt over her breasts.

"Oh, Lord, if that ain't a sight," moaned Collier. He whistled between his teeth and shook his head. "I'll be whipped if it's not!"

Jessie turned on him, color rising to her cheeks. "Damn it," she said tightly, "you *have* to do that, Collier?"

Nat Collier pushed back the brim of his hat and gave her a lopsided grin. "Reckon I just can't help myself, girl. You're 'bout the prettiest lady outlaw I ever did see."

Jessie jammed her hands on her hips and looked straight through him. "What is it, Collier? You figure if you keep on digging I'll fall down screaming and kicking—maybe ride off in tears and leave you alone? That's it, right?"

"Uh-huh. Something like that."

"Well, don't hold your breath!" Jessie said sharply. It was all she could do to keep from turning on her heel and stomping back to the beach. It was a pleasant evening and she could pull off her boots and walk along the shore, let the cool surf tug at her legs. When the sun went down she'd return, and Collier would be asleep...

"I'm damned if I will," she muttered stiffly. It was just what Nat Collier wanted, and she wasn't about to give him the satisfaction. Instead she squatted on her heels and filled a tin cup with boiling coffee, then spooned a plateful of the

1

cornbread and beans they'd had for breakfast. Moving back to her own side of the fire, she let the coffee cool and soaked the bread soft in the beans. A pair of brown pelicans flapped awkwardly overhead. White gulls screeched above the dunes, and Jessie tossed them a chunk of bread.

"We'll be getting there sometime tomorrow," said Nat. "'Spect they're gatherin' already, somewhere west of Victoria."

Jessie didn't look up. "You don't know where, though, do you?"

"I told you before, didn't I? Don't have to know *where*. If you got to have a map and an *en*-graved invitation, you sure ain't welcome in *that* bunch."

"Right. You told me," said Jessie.

"Got to tell a woman everything twice."

"Uh-huh. That's it, Nat." Once more, Jessie swallowed her anger. Collier wanted to fight, to drag her into an argument. He'd been at it from the moment they left Galveston, and he showed no sign of stopping. He was just like a bad-tempered hound, snapping at your heels every minute.

"You *say* you know what I'm talkin' about, but you don't," Collier grumbled to himself. "They want the likes of Billy Bonney and the James boys to show, they ain't going to put up signs. Word is maybe Clay Allison'll come. I tell you that? Jesus—now *there's* a number-one bastard!"

Jessie ignored him. Dropping the names of all the famous badmen he knew was one of Collier's favorite pastimes; it didn't much matter whether she was listening to him or not.

Collier finished his meal, belched, and tossed his plate away. Reaching in his pocket, he pulled out the butt of a cigarillo he'd been chewing all day, leaned to the fire, and puffed it into life.

Jessie watched him from the corner of her eye. He wasn't a bad-looking man—big, heavily fleshed all over, and none of it gone to fat. A good six-three, he was tall enough to carry his weight and use it. His face was country-solid, with a prizefighter's square-set jaw. Thick, sandy hair fell over his brow, framing dancing blue eyes and a boyish grin. A fine figure of a man, thought Jessie, if he wasn't simply

2

pure damn mean inside. She wondered, not for the first time, if Collier didn't play the outlaw role too well, enjoying it more than he should.

A chill touched her spine at the thought. *If you've got any doubts about that,* she told herself grimly, *what the hell are you doing out here?*

The darkened storeroom was nearly empty. Dirty kegs and boxes from the hardware store below lined the walls. The single kerosene lamp was turned low, adding more gloom than real light to the scene. Jessie stood again and paced to the window. The glass was nearly frosted from years of salt air; all she could see were dim halos of light from a nearby Galveston saloon. The sounds of a fiddle and a piano reached her ears, then a loud burst of laughter.

"Glad *someone's* having fun," she said darkly. Turning back to the room, she plopped down on a chair and stared at Ki. "You suppose anyone's coming? We must've been here nearly an hour."

Ki smiled from the shadows. "Closer to fifteen minutes, Jessie. They said they'd be here. They'll come."

"Good. I'm glad *you* think so. "I'm not all that certain."

"Patience calms the mind," he told her. "If you would take a deep breath and relax..."

"Oh, come on, Ki." Jessie shot him a narrow look. "I'm hot and tired and hungry and I need a bath bad. What I *don't* need right now is ancient Oriental wisdom."

Ki laughed and ran his fingers through his straight, raven-black hair. The dim light softened the sharp planes of his cheeks, the abrupt curve of his jaw, and the slightly tilted corners of his eyes. "It has nothing to do with Oriental wisdom, Jessie. It's simply the truth."

"Fine, I'll remind you of that next time you get the itch and start stomping around the room. Speaking of the itch—" Jessie stood and scratched violently at her waist. "If I don't find a tub of hot water soon, I'm going to start attracting flies."

"Outlaws don't take hot baths," Ki said solemnly.

"This one does. Just wait and see if she doesn't."

Ki sat up straight and shot her a glance as someone

3

muffled a cough down below. A moment later, two pairs of boots climbed the stairs. The storeroom door opened softly and the men walked in. One stayed in the shadow by the wall. The other glanced curiously at Ki, then let his eyes rest on Jessie.

"Miss Starbuck?" he said gruffly. "I'm Captain Simms, Texas Rangers. Mind if I take off my coat? It's plumb hot up here."

"Certainly, make yourself comfortable," said Jessie. She looked him over quickly and decided he fit the role. He was a big man in his fifties with a sun-weathered face and a shock of white hair under a high-crowned Stetson. A full silver mustache, yellowed by tobacco, hid a small, tight-lipped mouth, pursed in a permanent frown.

Simms took a handkerchief from his pocket, dusted off a keg, and sat down, holding his coat in his lap. "You don't mind, I'll get right to it," he said shortly. "I got to leave in an hour, and the trains don't wait." He paused and looked Jessie over for a long moment. "I'm going to be real frank, Miss Starbuck. I don't like bein' here, and I don't like you in this at all. You got some high-placed friends up in Austin, and I'm doin' what I'm told. Now—" He leaned forward and grabbed his thighs. "How much you know 'bout what's going on?"

"Just a minute please, Captain." Jessie brought herself erect and swept her bright amber hair off her shoulders. "Let *me* get something straight, all right? Those 'high-placed friends' you're talking about are sound, responsible men. They didn't send me down here 'cause I smiled real pretty and batted my eyes—which is exactly what you're thinking right now. I'm here because I can help. I didn't come to irritate you or anyone else."

The man by the wall gave a short little laugh. Jessie turned on him, her green eyes flashing. "Does your friend just stand there and giggle, Captain, or does he talk?"

Simms looked at Jessie without expression. "Right now, Miss Starbuck, he just stands there. And you didn't answer my question."

"How much do I know about this business?" Jessie let

4

out a breath. "The way I understand it, a large group of outlaws are gathering to the west, somewhere on the Nueces River. No one knows exactly why, but apparently it's something big. Your undercover man found a piece of a letter someone burned, and brought it to Ranger headquarters in Austin. He kept it because he thought it was a peculiar kind of letter to find in an outlaw fire. I saw that letter five days ago. There's not much left of it except a little writing in German that tells us nothing." She paused, and looked past Simms to the man in the shadow. "The important thing is the embossed crest at the top. A stylized crown. A friend who knows what it means showed it to me. It's the symbol of an international business cartel, Captain—an organization devoted to undermining this country. Stealing it blind and sucking it dry. I've crossed paths with them before, and that's why I'm here."

"What's why you're here, for Christ's sake!" The big man stepped forward out of shadow. He gave Jessie a look that undressed her on the spot, and she blushed in spite of herself. "I don't know a damn thing about any international whatever, but I *do* know what's coming off over there, lady. I been hanging out with that bunch two years. And I'm damned if I'm going to put *my* neck in a noose so some rich little—"

Ki came out of his chair. Jessie stopped him with a quick shake of her head.

"Collier!" Simms held up a hand and looked squarely at Jessie. "Collier, it's settled, damn it," he said harshly. "Talk straight or keep shut. I haven't got time for this."

Jessie looked up. "You're Nat Collier, then. The man who found the letter."

"That's not my name, but it's the only one you're going to hear."

Jessie stood, and looked from Collier to Simms. "It is *not* settled at all, Captain. If Mr. Collier will take me in, I think I can help. If the cartel's involved, they're in it for some good reason, I assure you. We're not talking about robbing a small-town bank or blowing a train. If I go in, maybe I can put my finger on the cartel's man."

"And maybe you can't," growled Collier.

Simms raised a brow. "You were about to tell me something, Miss Starbuck."

"Right, I was." She turned to face Collier. "Captain Simms thinks it's settled. I say it isn't. You're absolutely right. You've been undercover for two years. I won't ask you to risk your neck further. It's up to you, mister. You say no and I'm out."

Collier looked astonished. He stared at Jessie, then threw back his head and laughed out loud. "Well, I'll be a son of a bitch!"

"I sure won't argue that," Jessie said dryly.

Captain Simms chewed his lip. "You really mean that? It's up to Nat?"

"Of course I mean it."

"Well, then." Simms stood and almost smiled. "Looks like you're off the hook, fella."

"Hell no, I'm not, Cap'n." Collier's piercing blue eyes burned into Jessie's. She read the challenge plainly, and knew exactly what it meant. "Miss Starbuck an' me are going to get along just fine . . ."

Jessie walked a few yards from camp, watching the sun disappear below the flat Texas horizon. Evening turned the clouds blood red. She gazed past the waist-high stand of saltgrass toward the sea. Scrub-covered dunes gave way to the beach, and the darkening waters of Matagorda Bay. Past the calm inlet was the blur of Matagorda Island. Beyond it, the Gulf of Mexico vanished into the night.

She stood there a moment, then turned back to camp, smelling the sharp odor of burning coals and the beans Collier had dumped in the fire. *No use putting it off,* she thought glumly. *He's still going to be there, and you've got to sleep sometime . . .*

"Jessie—Jessie Starbuck!"

Jessie jerked around, startled. Her heart beat wildly against her breast and nearly stopped. Collier stood there in the dark, a big grin pasted on his face. "Damn it," Jessie said angrily, "is that your stupid idea of a joke?"

"Nope." Collier scratched his belly and shook his head.

6

"'Pears *you're* the joke, Miss Starbuck." His smile faded and his eyes went suddenly dark. "Shit, lady—what if one of them outlaws figures he seen you someplace before? You going to turn 'round and give him a pretty smile when he calls out your name? That's the oldest trick in the book. One minute you're smart an' got everybody fooled, the next you're deader'n hell."

Jessie bit her lip and looked at the ground. "I'm sorry. You're right, of course. Thanks, Collier."

"Don't thank me," he snorted. "I'm trying to stay alive. If you get caught, my goose is cooked 'long with yours."

"Yes. I know that." She looked at him, trying to see his features in the growing dark. "You want to tell me *why* you brought me, Collier? I can't figure that."

Collier laughed. "Lots of things you can't figure."

"No, I mean it."

"Maybe I just want to see what you'll do when the going gets rough." He spat on the ground and walked back to the fire. "Maybe I'm just out of my goddamn mind..."

Jessie turned over fitfully, tangling herself in the blanket. She was tired from the long day's ride, but sleep wouldn't come. She listened a moment to Collier's easy snoring. Pulling the blanket aside, she brushed out the sand as best she could. The south Texas sky blazed with stars. It was the middle of summer, but a welcome breeze blew in off the Gulf, keeping some of the giant mosquitoes at bay.

He's right, she thought. *I've got to know what I'm doing every minute, watch every word I say. I don't like the bastard, but I do owe him that.*

She reached up to slap something crawling down her neck and touched the unfamiliar texture of her hair. It was still a surprise to find her hair flat against her skull, parted in the middle and braided Indian-fashion on either side. It was dyed coal black, coarse and stiff now from the dust and the sun. She yearned to wash it, but that wouldn't do. She'd left Jessica Starbuck behind, and all that went with her—the well-tailored clothes, the tumble of strawberry-blonde hair that fell free over her shoulders. She was Sue Deevers now, at home in an old shirt and men's butternut

7

trousers a size too big. Not too far from the denims and shirt Jessica Starbuck wore for comfort, but far enough, she hoped. The battered gray hat and split Mexican serape helped the disguise, and even Nat Collier had grunted his approval.

The clothes and hair would help, she told herself, but inside was where it counted. She had to *be* Sue Deevers, not just *look* like her. *I'll either live the role or die in it,* she thought grimly. *Which it is is up to—*

Jessie cried out as his shadow suddenly loomed above her, blotting out the stars. She lashed out, clawing for his face. Strong hands slapped hers easily aside. His weight squeezed her flat, forcing the air out of her lungs. Jessie struggled, but his mouth ground roughly against hers, forcing her lips wide. She tasted tobacco and whiskey, smelled the acrid odor of his sweat. He straddled her quickly, one big hand gripping her wrists, the other tearing frantically at her shirt.

"You're my woman for now," he said hoarsely, "you by God better get used to it!"

"You had to try, didn't you?" Jessie said between her teeth. "Get the hell *off* me, damn you!"

Collier laughed. "I told you—you just didn't listen. I'm not trying, I'm *doing*. Been wantin' to get my hands on those pretty tits of yours since— Oh, Lord, ain't that nice!"

Jessie shrank back as he ripped the shirt away and bared her breasts. He gripped her flesh roughly in his hands, cupped one creamy sphere and squeezed hard.

Jessie gasped and threw her head from side to side. "Collier, please—don't!"

"Don't have to beg Nat Collier," he said softly. "I'm goin' to show you a time. Wait and see if I don't . . ."

Jessie closed her eyes and gritted her teeth. He held her arms tightly over her head as he buried his grizzled face against her breasts. His mouth roamed hungrily over the lush, swollen flesh. A moan escaped his lips as he drew her nipples into his mouth, kneading the hard buds between his teeth. She could feel the hardness at his groin pressed against her, his breath heaving faster in his chest. He suddenly pulled away, the skin drawn taut across his face.

"Let's get to the rest of it," he blurted. "I know you got

8

some sweet honey down there just for ol' Nat."

Jessie stared at him a moment, then laughed. "Hell, I'd rather get loved good than raped. You want to do it your way, or would you like a little help?"

Collier looked astonished, then a broad grin of pleasure crossed his features. "Damn, rich girls ain't any different from whores, now are they? Got your stove heated up some, didn't I?"

"Yeah, you did," Jessie admitted. "All right, damn it, a lot. Now get off me before you break something, and let me get out of these trousers."

Collier released her hands and sat back. Jessie rubbed her wrists and threw back the blanket, working at the buttons of her trousers.

"You're all right, you know? I mean that, girl." Collier's eyes flashed, taking in the firm tilt of her breasts, the sleek hollow of her abdomen.

"I'm better'n all right," Jessie purred. "Look what I got here for you darling..."

Inching her trousers down past the full curve of her hips, she slid one hand between her legs, then snaked it out fast and jammed the tiny derringer under his chin.

"Huh—what?" Collier's smile went flat. "Now just a damn minute—"

"Wrong," Jessie said sharply, pushing the twin barrels harder against his flesh. "A *second*, mister, that's all you've got. Any last requests?"

Collier blinked. "You wouldn't do it," he snorted. "I know damn well you wouldn't."

"You're right. I wouldn't. Not this time, anyway." Her green eyes bored into his. "Here it is, friend. You want to have your fun, go ahead and do it. Maybe you can sell them some kind of story they'll believe up in Austin. But make damned sure you kill me when you're finished. 'Cause if you don't, you're dead. Rape me and leave me alive and I'll shoot you the first chance I get. We understand each other?"

Collier studied her a long moment. His eyes told Jessie he believed her. "Yeah, all right. We got an understanding..."

9

"Fine." Jessie took the gun away from his chin and tossed it aside. "Now get the hell off me and let me get some sleep."

Collier cursed under his breath and stood up. He stared at her nearly naked form until she covered it with the blanket and turned away.

"Hell, you're all right," he said to her back. "You might just make it, Jessie."

"Sue," Jessie said flatly. "Sue Deevers. Try not to forget, Collier."

Chapter 2

Ki squatted on the bone-white rocks at the edge of the river, cupped his hands and scooped up the cool water and let it flow over his face and down his chest. His swaybacked horse grazed quietly on the shore just behind him, pulling up grass among the stones. The river was quiet, lined on either side with bright willows and tall cottonwoods. A crow flew overhead, spotted Ki, and squawked away.

Ki straightened, walked back and picked up the reins of his mount, and led it up the shallow hill. After he saddled the horse again, he tossed his saddlebag up behind, then hung the array of pots, kettles, skillets, and ladles over that. The horse turned and gave him a bleary-eyed look. Ki shrugged and slapped its neck.

"I apologize," he said gravely. "I don't like this any more than you do, friend."

For a long moment he stood in the shadow of the trees, studying the narrow dirt road running south. Then he mounted up and nudged the horse easily away from the river.

There was little traffic on the road. In the next five miles he met a Mexican farmer with a wagonload of melons, and a trader on a mule. Anyone who could avoid the midday heat was taking a nap somewhere, waiting for the sun to settle in the west.

Still, Ki slumped lazily in the saddle, for the benefit of anyone who happened his way. His hard, samurai-trained body was hidden under a shapeless cotton shirt and baggy trousers. The garments had been washed and patched until they had no color at all. The straight black hair that normally hung to his shoulders was pulled tight, knotted with a string at the base of his neck. A straw hat unraveling at the brim

11

covered his head, and his feet were dirty and bare. Anyone who noticed him would think he was one of the many anonymous Chinese of the West who worked as laundrymen and cooks. For the moment, that suited Ki fine.

As Ki passed the curve in the road, all his senses came alert. The sign nailed to a tree read VICTORIA and pointed to the south. The cluster of shacks rested just under the trees. Below was the ribbon of the Lavaca, brown and sluggish in the late months of summer. There was a corral and a weathered general store and cantina.

The roof of the cantina was patched with maguey-fiber matting to keep out the sun. Three men sat inside at a long plank table. As Ki came in sight, three pairs of eyes glanced up to look him over. He plodded past the cantina without stopping, keeping his eyes to the ground.

One quick sidelong look was all he needed. The horses lazing outside were strong and sturdy, built to eat up the miles. The saddlebags and rolled blankets were full, which told him the three were on the move. He'd read the men in an instant—hard, hollow-cheeked riders with nearly color-less eyes. If every man there wasn't wanted by the law, Ki would be very much surprised.

Leaving his horse at a hitching post, he walked up the steps and went inside. It was cool and dark, the shelves of the store lined with goods. There were the usual smells of onions and dried apples, but Ki noted another enticing odor over that—the tangy scent of chili-spiced stew.

"Yeah, you want something?"

Ki turned as a patch of white hair bobbed up from below the counter. He gave a careful little bow and looked at his feet. "I like supplies, please."

"You got cash money?" the man asked bluntly.

"Oh, yes." Ki's head bobbed up and down. "Have money to pay."

The man looked him over from head to toe, took Ki's short list, and turned to his shelves. He was a gaunt man in his sixties, with a deeply lined face and bushy brows. Dime-sized spectacles were perched on his nose.

"Sir," Ki asked politely, "I like some food, please, too. Stew smell good."

The man peered over his glasses, thought a moment, and made up his mind. "Go around out back," he said gruffly. "I can't serve you in here. And, uh—I'd stay away from them fellers in the bar if I was you."

Ki nodded gratefully and left. He didn't need the man's warning. No Oriental in his right mind would walk into a cantina in south Texas—not if he wanted to leave standing up.

Still, he had to get close to the men somehow, put them at ease with his presence. He was almost certain they were headed for the outlaw gathering. Collier had said the meeting would take place somewhere to the west of Victoria, along the Nueces River. Well, he was nearly there. The gear on the nag out front said he was a cook as plain as day. All he could do now was wait.

There was a chopping stump out back, near a large stack of firewood. He could hear the men in the bar, not twenty feet to his left. From the sound of them, they'd had plenty to drink already.

A screen door slammed and Ki looked up. A young girl ran down the steps, balancing a kettle of stew and a stack of bowls. She disappeared quickly into the cantina, but not before Ki got a good look. She was young and pretty, with flashing brown eyes and a thick head of coal-black hair. Her frayed gingham dress clung to an incredibly slim waist and the youthful tilt of her breasts.

Suddenly the girl screamed. Crockery shattered on the table and the men howled with laughter. Ki came up off his stump, then caught himself and took a deep breath. No, that wouldn't do. Chinese cooks didn't poke their noses into white men's business.

In a moment the girl appeared again, anger in her eyes and a flush on her cheeks. The sleeve of her dress was torn, baring honeyed flesh to the shoulder. She bolted into the kitchen, came out, and handed Ki his stew, then left without looking at him twice.

Ki dunked a slice of hot bread in his stew and ate it with

13

relish. The beef was stringy, but there were plenty of potatoes and slices of hot pepper. When the girl appeared again, he watched her from under his hat as she carried a fresh bottle to the cantina.

The old man's crazy, Ki thought to himself. *Keeping a girl like that around here is like waving a red flag in front of a bull.*

Almost at once the girl shrieked again. This time there was real pain in her voice. A man shouted in anger and Ki heard the slap of a hand against flesh.

Easy, easy now . . . Ki clenched his fists and sat tight.

The old man came out of the door, his face the color of ash. He stared toward the saloon, bit his lip, and ducked back inside. The girl whimpered like a puppy. The sound of ripping fabric reached Ki's ears. The girl sobbed, and the men sighed in appreciation.

"Goddamn," one said hoarsely, "that is mighty fine-lookin' stuff."

"Oh, Lord, no—*please!*" the girl begged. Someone slapped her again and she gasped for breath.

Ki tossed the stew aside and walked quickly around the corner to the cantina.

The men looked up, startled, surprise turning quickly to anger. A heavyset man with sandy hair glared at Ki.

"Damn it, Chinaman—what the *hell* you doin' in here?"

"Yes. Sorry." Ki grinned foolishly and stepped back, clasping his hands together.

The girl stared at him with glazed and frightened eyes. An ugly welt colored her cheek. She was spread-eagled atop the table; the gown was torn to her belly and bundled at her waist. Ki caught a flash of pointed breasts, long legs, and naked thighs.

The big man caught Ki's glance, and his mouth curled in a grin. "Just come in to take a peek, did you? Christ, that ain't too good a idea, chink."

The other men laughed, knowing what was coming.

"Hank, let's see if he's got a yellow pecker," a bearded man called out. The remark brought another burst of laughter.

The man called Hank looked solemnly at Ki. "What you

14

say, friend? Is Willy right about that? You got a chink pecker?"

"I—do not understand." Ki shook his head and tried to look bewildered.

"Yeah, sure you do." Hank's smile faded. His hand went to his belt and came up with a single-action Colt. The hammer clicked back under his thumb, and the muzzle touched the cheekbone under Ki's left eye. "Now. Take your trousers down, boy. Let's see what color it is."

Ki saw exactly how it would happen. His left would come up fast and send the weapon flying. Before the man could blink, his right hand would drive through the throat and crush the windpipe flat. Half a second later he'd stop the bearded man's heart with his foot, whip about, and catch the third man across the bridge of the nose . . .

"Come on, damn it," Hank said harshly, "Don't you hear good, chink?"

"I want no trouble. Please." Ki let his eyes go wide. "I help you." He nodded past the barrel of the gun. "With girl . . ."

Hank's jaw fell. He lowered the Colt and burst out laughing. "You're going to *what*? Christ A'mighty, you hear that, Willy? Chink here thinks you need help!"

"I'll help the bastard," snarled Willy. He let go of the girl and started for Ki, fists knotted at his sides.

"Wait—please!" Ki held up his hands. "No hurt me. I help. Give good medicine, after you pleasure woman. You see, is *good* medicine. Fine Chinese herbs!"

Willy came to a halt. He squinted at Ki and glared back at the girl. "Christ, what are you talkin' about? I don't *need* no medicine."

"No," Ki explained. "Not now. *After* pleasure." Ignoring Hank's weapon, he took a step forward. "Girl is very pretty. Make nice loving for you. But she is sick, you see?"

"What—what kinda sick?" Hank asked narrowly.

"Sickness man and woman get *here*," Ki said softly, lightly touching his groin.

Willy stared. "You mean she's got the—" He stopped, and looked sharply at Ki. "How the hell do *you* know what she's got?"

15

"Is all here, sir," Ki said patiently, pointing at his own eyes. "Pupil very dark. Too large. Whites are yellow. Veins broken." Ki knew his description was accurate. The girl was scared to death and she'd been crying.

Willy scratched his head and looked at the girl. She'd drawn up her legs and pulled the tattered dress about her as best she could. The gown was nearly in ribbons, and a great deal of enticing flesh was still bare.

"She looks damn good to me," growled Willy. "There ain't *nothin'* wrong with this little gal."

"Well, then, get you some of it," Hank urged with a grin.

Willy looked at Hank, then turned to the man in the corner. "How 'bout you, Barc? You ain't listening to the chink, are you?" The man hadn't spoken since Ki had entered the room. He was older than the others, likely close to forty, a man with broad, flat features and lazy eyes.

"Do what you like," he said flatly, "but get at it fast. We're leavin' here in 'bout ten minutes."

Willy frowned, glanced longingly at the girl, then turned on his heel and knocked Ki flat. Ki saw him coming and went with the blow, letting the big fist roll off his jaw. He crashed into the wall and bellowed in pain, covering his head and chest against the man's boots. Willy picked him up by the shirt, held him out straight, and hit him again. Ki's head snapped back. Willy hit him solidly in the belly and folded him up.

Ki took it, covering himself as best he could and making no effort at all to fight back. Part of his training had been in learning to take blows as brutal as these. Finally he feigned unconsciousness and sank to the floor. He lay there and listened to the men's laughter and the heavy clumping of the men's boots as they stomped out of the cantina, and then the softer pattering of the girl's feet as she ran out the back door, sobbing.

He shook his head and spat blood, then brought himself painfully to his knees. He could hear the men outside, walking their mounts around the yard, calling to one another. Carefully he tried his arms and legs, biting back the pain. Willy's big fists had worked him over, but he was still in

16

one piece. It had taken all he had to let the man hit him over and over again. And damn it, all for nothing, too! He was beat all to hell and not a step closer to getting himself into the outlaw camp. He couldn't let Jessie just—

Ki froze as the shadow fell over his face. He looked up quickly and saw the rough features of the man named Barc.

"You all right, Chinaman?"

"I am fine." Ki nodded.

Barc grinned. "That girl. She really got the clap?"

"Oh, yes. Worse than that, sir."

Barc spat on the ground, inches from Ki's head. "You're probably lying. Worked with Chinamen before on the railroad, and never seen one yet that didn't lie." He paused, and Ki looked away, knowing the man would expect it. "All those pans and shit you got on your horse—you really a cook, or you just doctor whores?"

"I am cook. Very *good* cook, sir." Ki attempted a smile.

"You lookin' for work?" He saw the hesitation in Ki's eyes and shook his head. "Willy won't hurt you. Not 'less I tell him to."

"Then I am looking for work," said Ki.

"Good," Barc grunted. "Be down at the crossing tomorrow afternoon. Know where it is? 'Bout eight miles south."

"I will find it," said Ki.

"Better get something for that face," said Barc. "Don't want you scaring hell outa my boys." He turned then and stalked outside. Ki didn't move until he heard the horses ride away . . .

Chapter 3

Ki made his way to the pump behind the store, stripped off his shirt, and poured water over his head. Passing his fingers gingerly over his body, he winced at the points of pain. His ribs were badly bruised, and the big outlaw had scraped his face raw.

It worked, though, he told himself grimly. *I've got a ticket inside . . .*

"You all right, boy? Damn, I thought they'd killed you for sure."

Ki straightened at the old man's voice. "Yes. I am fine. Thank you."

"Christ. You don't *look* fine." The man made a face and handed Ki a handful of clean rags. "Fool thing to do, you know. Told you to leave those bastards alone."

"Yes." Ki dried his face and lowered his eyes. "I was foolish, as you say."

The old man shuffled and looked at his feet. "Listen, I—appreciate what you done," he said hesitantly. "I got no room for you inside, but you're welcome to bunk out in the barn. It's kinda late to be traveling."

"I am grateful," said Ki. "I will accept your kind offer." He folded the cloths on the pump and shook out his shirt. "The young woman—she is not hurt badly?"

The man's face went hard. "That's no business of yours, now is it?" Muttering under his breath, he turned and left Ki standing in the yard.

The barn was no more than a shed attached to the corral, but there was plenty of dry straw. Before the sun went down,

18

he forced himself to walk through the trees to the bank of the river. His body protested, but he knew what happened to bruised muscle and tendon. If he babied himself too much, he'd stiffen up worse the next day.

Back at the shed, he settled in gratefully on a deep pile of straw. Through the loosely thatched roof he watched the bright points of stars. A hot wind stirred the branches overhead and sent an owl flying.

He wondered how Jessie was faring, and what she was doing at the moment. Ki hadn't liked the idea of sending her off with Nat Collier. He didn't like Collier any more than Collier liked him. Still, Jessie was determined to get in the outlaw camp, and Collier was likely the only way. Ki had argued that it would be a lot easier simply to find the outlaw camp and get word back to the Rangers, Jessie, of course, was well aware that Ki knew better than that. Locking up a bunch of gunslingers would serve no purpose at all. The cartel would just lie low and try the same scheme somewhere else—and be a lot more careful.

Ki sat up immediately at the sound. Peering into the darkness, he saw the pale figure move quietly across the yard toward the shed. When he saw it was the girl, he relaxed.

"Are you in there?" she whispered. "Is it all right if I come in?"

"Yes," Ki told her, "of course." He started to rise, and the girl held up a hand.

"No, just sit still, please. You don't have to do that." She knelt down in the straw, rustling it with her skirts. "I brought you a slice of ham and some biscuits. You didn't exactly finish up supper."

Ki accepted the covered dish with a nod. "Thank you. I am very grateful. You are all right, I hope?"

"I'll live," she sighed. "Thanks to you. Are you hurt real bad?"

"No. Not hurt bad. Be better in...one day."

The girl leaned forward intently, straining to see him in the dark. "Listen, you don't have to keep doing that, you know. Not in front of me."

Ki's stomach tightened. "Keep doing what?"

19

"Talking pidgin Chinese," she said bluntly, "or whatever it is that's supposed to be. I'm a ship captain's daughter, and I grew up on the San Francisco wharves. I've seen every kind of Oriental there is, and you are *not* Chinese. You're not all Japanese, either. Which was it? Your mother, most likely."

Ki was taken aback. "My mother, yes. My father was American." He shook his head and looked at her with concern. "I'm glad I did better with those three than I did with you."

The girl laughed at his expression, then her pleasant smile faded. "I don't know why you're pretending to be something you're not. That's none of my business. But I wouldn't worry if I were you. Most white people can't tell the difference between one Oriental and another. But I'm not telling *you* anything new. Just watch out for girls who grew up around ships."

"I will," Ki replied. "I have learned a valuable lesson."

"See? You've got a real nice voice when you're talkin' like yourself." She held out a hand and Ki took it. "My name's Marcie Brewer, by the way. Don't guess I said so, did I?"

"And I am—Muto," he said, giving her the first Japanese name he could think of. "And the old man in the store?"

"My grandfather. Don't mind him. He's been real good to me, but—well, he's not too friendly. Doesn't like people all that much." She seemed to guess his thoughts, and looked away. "He takes care of me as good as he can. Really. It's just—all the fight's gone out of him. Guess that happens sometimes."

"Yes. I guess it does."

Marcie was silent a long moment. "You'll be leaving in the morning?"

Ki nodded. "There is something I must do."

"Then—would you—I mean—" She took a deep breath and looked right at him. "Damn it, is it all right if I stay out here with you tonight? I don't know any other way to say it!"

Ki stared. It wasn't often he missed the gleam in a woman's eye, but Marcie Brewer had taken him by surprise. "Uh, yes—of course you can stay," he said dryly, "I'd be—"

Marcie grinned and scooted herself close to him on the hay. Reaching her arms around his neck, she kissed him lightly on the mouth. "You don't have to be shocked," she said softly. "I'm just a girl who needs some loving, Muto. Most of the men who stop here are like the ones you saw today. If they *don't* try to rape you, they're sure as hell thinking about it. And Grandpa chases off all the nice ones..."

Ki slipped his hands around her waist and drew her to him. Marcie shuddered at his touch and came eagerly into his arms. Ki kissed her eyes and the softness of her cheek, breathing in the fresh, clean smell of her hair. Marcie's mouth went slack, and he gently touched the corner of her lips with his tongue. With a sigh, she brought her mouth up hungrily to meet his. Ki explored each warm and secret hollow, drinking in the sweet taste of her mouth. He let his lips trail the column of her neck, burrowing into the feathery curls about her ears. Marcie sucked in a breath and held him tightly. Ki slid his hands up from her waist and pressed his thumbs gently over the tips of her breasts. Firm little nipples sprang up to meet his touch, straining against the thin cotton cloth. A low moan caught in Marcie's throat. Her fingers came up to sweep Ki's aside and tear at the buttons of her bodice. Ki helped her slip the cotton blouse off her shoulders, then loosened her arms from the sleeves. In an instant she was bare to the waist. Ki marveled at her pale, creamy flesh, the taut swell of her breasts. He reached up to touch her, and Marcie held him back.

"No," she whispered, "not yet. Get me all naked first. I want you to look at me."

"I can't think of anything I'd rather do more," Ki told her. She gave him an impish smile and tossed her dark hair over her shoulders. Ki slipped his hands around her waist, and Marcie raised her bottom to let him slide her skirt down her hips and over her legs. She kicked her toes free and sent the skirt flying. Ki reached out to draw her to him, and

Marcie laughed and rolled away, then sprang to her feet and grinned.

Ki looked puzzled. "Ah, just where do you think you're going?"

"I *said* I wanted you to look at me, remember? You can't do that if I'm over there with you."

"I could sure as hell try," he protested.

Marcie laughed again and took a step forward, stretching one slim leg ahead of the other. Resting her hands on her hips, she threw back her shoulders and thrust out her breasts. The motion hollowed her belly and tightened the flesh over her ribs. When the pale light of the stars touched her body, Marcie's unblemished skin seemed to glow with a light of its own.

"My God, you're right," Ki said softly. "You are something worth seeing, Marcie."

"You like me all right?" she teased. "You're sure, now?"

"Very sure," said Ki. "Now why don't you just—"

"My breasts aren't too big," she said soberly. "But I guess they'll do, huh?"

"They are—lovely," Ki said dryly. "They'll do just fine."

"They *say* you can make 'em some bigger," Marcie whispered. "You just kinda—rub 'em real good, and—and draw your fingers up easy like—oh, yes! Like that. Like . . . that . . ."

Ki stared, and felt his manhood stiffen even more. Marcie's full lips went slack. Her dark eyes held him, watching him intently as her fingers made slow, lazy circles over her breasts. She cupped the hard little mounds between her hands, pressing them as gently as a lover. As Ki watched, her palms slid over her flesh and came together, until she held each nipple between her fingers. She squeezed the firm nubs, let her fingers relax, then softly squeezed again. Without taking her eyes off Ki, she took a step toward him and went to her knees. Her face was only inches from his own. She held each nipple up high, and gave him a saucy grin.

"If you like hard and pointy little tits," she said gently, "I reckon maybe these are all ready. You think you'd like to—*ahhhhhh!*"

Ki clutched her waist in both hands, lifted her off her knees, and dropped her in the hay. Marcie gasped and tossed

22

her long legs in the air. Ki quickly stepped out of his trousers and pulled his loose cotton shirt over his head. Marcie's eyes went wide at the sight of his erection.

"Lord a'mercy," she gasped. "Guess you were watchin' real good!" The pink tip of her tongue flicked out to wet her lips. She brought herself up to her knees again and ran her fingers over his thighs. He could feel her hands tremble as she cupped his member gently on the tips of her fingers. Raising her head, she looked at him and smiled, then let her tongue trail softly around the head of his shaft. Ki felt himself swell at her touch. A tumble of dark hair brushed his belly. Her lips moved smoothly around him, caressing him with her warmth. Ki closed his eyes and let out a breath. Marcie's fingers clutched his hips as her tongue explored his length. She teased him, nipped him gently with her teeth. The tip of her tongue slid lazily along the underside of his member. Again and again, she stroked him with the furnace of her mouth. Ki felt the storm raging within him, racing through his loins. Marcie sensed his excitement and raked her nails across his flesh. Ki brushed her hair aside and looked at her face. She was flushed, her cheeks sucked hollow with desire. Her mouth moved faster and faster until her brow slammed hard against his belly. Ki felt his swelling grow, and knew he could hold back his pleasure no longer. White heat thundered through his body with a strength that made him shudder. Marcie moaned with delight as he exploded into her mouth. She stroked him with her lips, eagerly drinking him in. Even when he filled her, she refused to let him go. Her tiny cries of hunger pressed hard against his thighs, until Ki reached down and took her gently in his arms.

She lay in the hollow of his shoulder, dark eyes focused on some point beyond the thatched roof of the shed. A sliver of new moon dappled the hay and turned her flesh a buttery gold. Ki marveled at her touch, the slender lines of her body. Marcie was young, he knew, barely seventeen. Still, she was clearly already a woman, despite her coltish legs and her breasts as hard as apples. He moved his free hand to touch her, sliding his fingers up the shadow of her belly to circle her breasts.

23

"Ah, yes," Marcie moaned, "that is *real,* real fine . . ."

"Good," Ki said solemnly. "If that gives you pleasure, perhaps you'll enjoy this as well." He took her nipple between two fingers and stroked it gently.

"Mmmmmmm, my, yes. Oh, dear!" She purred into his cheek and kissed his shoulder. "Think maybe you're right. I *do* enjoy that."

"Fine. You are supposed to."

"I am, huh?" Marcie twisted out of his grasp and scooted her head up on his chest. "Guess you know just 'bout all there is to know about girls, right?"

"No," Ki said soberly, "I do not. Any man who tells you that, Marcie, is both a liar and a fool."

"But you do know *some* things, don't you?"

"Yes. I am happy to say I do."

"I'll bet." She grinned and came up on her elbows, cupping her chin in her palms. "I don't know much about men. Not really."

Ki gave her a narrow look. "I could argue with that, Marcie."

"Well . . ." She gave him a little girl shrug. "I know some. Like I told you, fellows come by now and then. And Grandpa don't run 'em *all* off." She reached over and planted a kiss on his mouth. "You're a nice man, you know that? I'm sure glad you came by. Hell, for more reasons than one. You got me out of a lot of trouble." She giggled and touched his nose. "And *in* some, too, I guess."

"I'm not through yet, either," Ki told her.

Marcie laughed, then her smile suddenly faded. "You're leaving in the morning."

"Yes. I have to, Marcie."

"Know you can't take me with you—and hey, I'm not even asking," she added quickly. "Lord God, I'm going to be stuck in South Texas forever!"

"I don't believe that."

"No? Why not?"

"Someone will take you out of here, Marcie. A girl like you—"

"Is what?" Marcie pouted and gave him a look. "Pretty? A good roll in the hay? Hell, there's thousands of girls can

24

do that. How'm I any different, damn it?" Suddenly, tears filled her eyes. "Go on, tell me. Just how?"

Ki took her in his arms and buried her cries against his shoulder. Marcie clung to him; her hands clawed at his back; her body trembled with a fear and desperation that quickly turned to hunger. Through her tears came the small animal cries of a deeper need. The shudders that wrenched her slender frame slowed to an easy rhythm, a motion that flowed from her breasts past her belly to the nest between her thighs.

Ki pressed her to him, letting his erection grind firmly against the high mound of her pleasure. Marcie's breath came in quick, hot bursts against his shoulder. He took her breasts between his lips, drawing the tender nipples into his mouth. Marcie gave a harsh little cry and spread her legs wide. The heady woman-smell of her assailed Ki's senses and heightened his excitement. Pulling away from her embrace, he reached down to part the moist petals between her thighs. Marcie groaned and thrust herself up to meet him.

"Please," she sobbed. "Please, I— Oh, God, get inside me. I *need* you inside me!"

"I know," he whispered, "it's all right, Marcie. It's all right . . ."

Ki entered her slowly, sliding his member into the warmth of her flesh. Marcie gave a strangled little cry and her legs whispered around him, urging him deeper still. Ki thrust harder, and Marcie matched his strokes. The proud mound of her pubis kissed his loins. She kneaded him with soft, velvety flesh, drawing his rigid shaft into her body. Her hard breasts ground against him, the hot points of her nipples feeling as if they might burn his chest. Her legs gripped his hips, and her back arched far off the ground.

Ki felt himself climbing toward a thundering peak of pleasure. He grasped the slender circle of her waist, plunging himself deeper and deeper inside her. Marcie's breathing matched the pounding of his shaft. A growing heat raced through his body, crying for release. Marcie felt him swell inside her and gave a final gasp of joy. Her encircling flesh spasmed against him, drawing him closer and closer to the edge.

25

Ki threw back his head; the muscles in his face went taut. With a ragged gasp he exploded inside her. His orgasm triggered hers, loosing the fires within her. Her body went stiff, and for a long moment she hung on the crest of her pleasure. Finally she went limp beneath him, the sleek flesh of her legs falling away, her arms dropping slowly to her sides.

Marcie stared up at him out of the darkness. Her hair clung to her face, and bright pearls of moisture beaded her cheeks.

"Oh, Lordy," she whispered, "I feel a whole lot better'n I did!"

Ki grinned. "Yes, so do I. You are a very lovely woman, Marcie. Truly."

"You're kinda lovely yourself," she told him. Her black eyes held him. "I'm sure as hell going to miss you. Maybe—maybe you'll be coming back through sometime..."

"Maybe I will," he said. "I'd like that." It was true, though he knew he'd likely never see her again.

"Guess I'd better be gettin' back inside," she sighed. "Grandpa's a pretty sound sleeper, but if he ever wakes up and finds me gone..."

"Yes. That wouldn't do."

She rose then, and the sight of her slim young figure stirred him again. He stood and helped her into the gown.

"You take care of yourself now," he told her.

"You do the same," she whispered, stretching up to kiss him. "And watch out for girls with—you know, *terrible* diseases and such."

Ki smiled and held her. "Yes, I'll do that."

"You can tell by looking in their eyes," she said soberly. "I think I heard that somewhere."

"Yes, you can tell a great deal from the eyes," he said gently. "That much is very true, Marcie..."

Chapter 4

Nat Collier reined in his mount, stepped down, walked a few paces, and sniffed the air. He turned then and nodded abruptly to Jessie, and she swung out of the saddle to join him. The day was steaming hot, without a breeze, but the massive oaks offered shade. They left the horses and walked through the trees toward the west. Finally Collier held up a hand and stopped, motioning Jessie up beside him.

"Down there." He pointed. "That river's the Guadalupe. We wait right here."

Jessie gave him a curious look. "What for? Why don't we go on?"

Collier's smile twisted. "'Cause we don't know where the hell we're going. Not till someone comes and tells us. Jesus Christ, woman—"

Jessie swallowed her anger. "I just asked, Collier. I don't know everything."

"Now that is the God's truth," he muttered. He walked off then and vanished into the trees. In a moment she heard water splattering off a rock, and knew the noise was for her benefit.

Jessie shook her head and glanced out over the river. He hadn't let up a minute on the ride north from the coast. Usually it was something about rich ranchers' daughters, or women messing in things that didn't concern them. Just where *did* he think women belonged, Jessie had asked him, and Collier gladly told her: in the bed, in the kitchen, and bent over the washtub. Period. Any time they ventured further than that, they got their pretty asses in trouble.

We're going to make a lovely pair in that outlaw camp,

27

she thought grimly. *Badman Collier and his friendly little whore . . .*

Collier stomped out of the trees, making a big show of buttoning his trousers. "Better get that stuff unloaded and gather up some wood," he told her. "We'll likely be stayin' here for supper."

"Gather it up yourself," Jessie snapped.

Collier turned on her, his blunt features twisted in rage. The back of his hand came up fast and caught her across the face. Jessie hit the ground hard and raised a hand to her cheek. Collier stood over her, his fists clenched at his sides.

"Now listen to me," he growled, "and listen good, lady. Just because you pulled that little peashooter on me don't mean shit. I'll strip you naked and have you right here if the mood happens to hit me. So don't let *that* go to your head. It ain't goin' to work for you but once."

"Collier—"

"Shut up, damn it! What I'm talkin' about don't have nothing' to do with you and me on a blanket. We're goin' to have company soon—and when we do, we better look good. That means Nat Collier and Sue Deevers. You cookin' supper and haulin' wood and movin' your ass when I tell you." He paused and gave her a sly grin. "And lookin' like you're plain fuckin' crazy about bein' my woman. Those bastards figure anything else—" He let the rest of the words die.

Jessie pulled herself erect. "All right, damn it." Her green eyes bored into his. "But don't you ever hit me again, Collier. You do, and I'll play your Sue Deevers right to the hilt. You ever hear of an outlaw whore killin' her man?"

Collier threw back his head and laughed. "Get a fire goin' woman. My belly feels like a barrel full of nothin' . . ."

They came down the path along the far side of the river in late afternoon, four men trailing single file, the girl clinging to the saddle of the leader. They stopped there, and Collier stepped into the open and waved. The leader waved back, and motioned the others across the shallows.

Jessie glanced up from her fire and watched them ride into camp. Three of the men were young, barely in their

28

twenties, but all bore the hollow-eyed look of men used to covering their trail. The girl was slim and pretty. She was Mexican, no more than fifteen, and clearly frightened to death. Her simple black dress was torn at the shoulder, and there was an ugly bruise on her cheek.

It was the leader, though, who caught Jessie's eyes and held them. He stepped down from the saddle and greeted Collier, and for an instant his glance touched Jessie. She shuddered and stirred her beans. Lord God, the man looked like a snake peeled out of his skin! He was as thin as a rail, all planes and bony angles. His face was pasty white and drained of blood—like something that lived in a hole and never saw the light of day.

"Susie," Collier bellowed, "get on over here, honey!"

Jessie started, then remembered who she was. Setting the food off the fire, she walked up lazily to Collier and his friend, dropping a hand to her hip. Collier grinned and gave her a wink.

"This here's Susie, Dutch. Ain't she somethin'?"

Dutch didn't smile. His clothes hung on him like rags on a stick. The long-barreled Smith & Wesson in his belt looked much too heavy for his frame, but Jessie was certain he knew how to use it.

"Where'd you get her?" he said flatly. "Godammit, Nat—"

"Now, hell, don't worry 'bout her." Collier shook his head and shrugged. "Me and Susie been together a long spell. Shit, I ain't no fool."

The pale blue eyes looked her over, stripping her naked where she stood. "Where you from, girl?"

"Galveston, New Orleans—wherever I *want* to be from," Jessie said boldly.

The narrow slash of a mouth curled at the corners. "Got a tongue on you, I see. You do anything with it 'sides talking?"

Jessie forced a sleepy smile. "Reckon I can handle what I need to, mister."

"That's for goddamn sure," Collier boasted. He gripped Dutch's arm and turned him around. "Come on, get off your feet. I got some good Irish in my pack. Jesus, where'd you

29

find the Mex? She sure is a perky little thing."

Dutch moved off and didn't look at her again. Jessie breathed a sigh of relief and walked back to her fire. In a moment, two of the young men sauntered over and she served them bacon and bread and nodded at the coffee. They took their plates without speaking, and walked back to the trees. When the third boy wandered in, Jessie stopped him.

"What about the girl?" she asked. "You taking anything to her?"

The boy turned, showing her a patch of yellow hair and one glazed eye. "She ain't hungry," he said flatly.

"How do *you* know?" Jessie asked bluntly. "You ask her if she was?"

"Don't have to ask her nothing," the boy muttered. He snatched the plate from Jessie, spat in the fire, and walked away. Nat came up behind him, shot Jessie a warning look, and took a plate for himself and the man called Dutch.

When the men were finished, she took the plates to the river and scrubbed them with sand, then started back to the camp. Halfway there she heard the scream. Jessie froze in her tracks, the terrible sound chilling her to the bone. She knew what they were doing, and that she was helpless to do anything to stop it. She swallowed hard to keep down her supper, and climbed wearily up the slope.

The men laughed back in the trees. The girl gave a long, ragged cry and went silent. Nat walked into the open and stood over Jessie.

"Get the stuff packed," he said shortly. "We're ridin' out while there's still plenty of light."

Jessie stared at him. "You have her too, Collier?"

Collier's face went rigid. "No, goddammit, I didn't. Don't guess you believe that, do you?"

"Yeah, I believe you. Sorry I asked. Is she—is she all right, Nat?"

Collier's face fell. "Jesus Christ, no. Of course she's not all right!" He turned quickly and walked off toward the horses. When they rode down the path to the river after Dutch and his men, the Mexican girl wasn't with them.

After a good half hour they left the river and turned west.

30

Collier rode beside Jessie awhile, then spurred his mount to join Dutch. Before he left he told Jessie that Dutch had informed him the outlaws were gathering at the camp. A hundred or so were there already, and more were riding in all the time. The summer light would hold for some while, and Collier figured they'd get to the camp by dark.

"We'd better," he said shortly, "or the bastards won't let us in. They're plenty goddamn itchy, and I guess they got reason. Doc Holliday's there, and Clay Allison hisself. Dutch says the word is Jesse and Frank are coming."

"My God," Jessie whispered.

"Didn't believe me, did you?" said Collier. "That's it, isn't it?"

"Oh, I believe you," said Jessie. "I just can't see men like that taking such a chance, even if the cartel's money *is* behind this business. What are they going to steal, Nat? California?"

"More'n likely," he grunted. "And a couple of territories to boot."

Jessie rode alone at the rear of the column. The hot ball of the sun was low in the west, coloring the sky brassy yellow and stretching long shadows over the land. Jessie earnestly wished Ki were with her now, riding along beside her. Was he there already? Ahead, in the outlaw camp? She knew his chances of getting inside were far slimmer than her own. Still, she had all the confidence in the world that he'd make it. Ki wasn't about to let her go in there alone. He'd made that perfectly clear.

She squinted against the sun, her thoughts moving ahead to the outlaw camp. What was the cartel after this time? she wondered. Whatever it was, the prize had to be enormous. The men gathering there wouldn't risk their lives for nothing—and the cartel never shared its riches without a reason. She and Ki had learned that lesson more than once.

Suddenly Jessie's memories swept farther west, to a grave on the Starbuck ranch. Her father lay there in the earth, not far from where the cartel's assassins had gunned him down. It was a moment that had changed Jessie's life, wrenching her abruptly into a world she'd never imagined even existed.

As a young girl, she'd only guessed at the troubles that plagued her father. Just before his death, he'd told her the staggering truth about the men he'd fought half his life. She learned how he'd come up against them as a young man, building a trade empire across the Pacific to Japan. The powerful European cartel wanted the riches of the Orient for themselves, and didn't intend to share them with any others. Alex Starbuck had fought back, and the fight raged across Europe and America. The cartel murdered Jessie's mother, and Alex took his revenge. Finally the faceless leaders of the cartel sent their assassins to kill Starbuck himself, on his own Texas ranch. After the murder, Jessie, as her father's only child, had inherited the vast Starbuck holdings, and the terrible responsibility that went with them. It was a responsibility she could easily have denied—she was young, and a woman besides. No one would have faulted her for backing away. Instead she chose to take up her father's fight, to take it wherever it might lead.

Only it leads nowhere at all, Jessie thought grimly. *It winds in a circle, like a snake twisting back on itself. There's no end, no end at all . . .*

Jessie blinked and pulled her mount aside as the riders ahead came to a halt. The sun was gone behind blood-red clouds. Jessie stood in the saddle. There was nothing to see except a line of dusty scrub. Collier rode back beside her and stopped.

"We're here," he said tightly. "Just keep quiet and do as you're told."

"Doesn't look to me like we're anywhere at all," said Jessie.

Collier made a face. "It ain't supposed to look like Chicago or something, now is it? Just stick close to ol' Nat, and you'll be just fine."

"Yeah, that makes me feel a whole lot better," Jessie said shortly.

Collier grinned and showed his teeth. "I'm probably out of my damn mind, bringin' you in here, you know? You'll likely get us *both* killed." He reached over quickly and pinched her belly, then kicked his mount and rode back to his companions.

Chapter 5

From the moment they left Galveston and started west, Jessie had formed a picture in her mind of the outlaw camp. A cavern, maybe—there were plenty of those around. Or a high escarpment in the rough hill country farther north, a place at the end of a blind canyon where well-placed marksmen could hold off an army. Instead she found herself following Collier and the others through the scrub and down the hill to a thick stand of oaks and tall pecans. The trees were on the flats beside a river, forming a natural camping ground. Tents and lean-tos of every shape and size were spread about, and evening cookfires were burning.

Jessie took in the scene at a glance. An image came to mind nearly at once, and it was all she could do to keep from laughing. What it looked like was an old-fashioned revival meeting by the river!

She shook her head in wonder, knowing that was exactly what the outlaws had in mind. Guards out in the brush would make certain that strangers kept their distance. If anyone did get curious about this gathering in the wilds, a friendly "brother" would explain how his sect liked to worship the Lord in peace. That ought to do it, Jessie decided. Everyone respected another man's religion.

Outlaws glanced up to watch her pass, and hooted and made lewd remarks. Nat Collier stopped them with a look. He found a spot well away from the others, got off his horse, and handed the reins to Jessie.

"Set up our stuff over there," he said quietly. "Anyone bothers you, just ignore 'em. And don't get friendly with *no* one, hear?"

"And where'll you be?"

"Dutch is takin' me over to meet the big cheese," Collier replied with a scowl. "I been ridin' with some of these fellers, but the folks runnin' this show are real touchy. You ain't exactly in till they *say* you're in."

Jessie nodded and glanced past him. "Looks to me like we're in for sure, Nat."

"Uh-huh." Collier understood what she was saying. "You like to try an' ride *out*, I'll stand here an' watch..."

Jessie took the horses to the communal corral by the river, then walked back to set up camp. There wasn't much to do; Collier didn't have a tent, only a canvas tarp that could be set up as a lean-to where they could huddle if it rained. She set that up by a tree, laid their blankets and gear aside, and started a fire. The beans were hot and the salt bacon sizzling when she looked up and saw the girl walking toward her. She was pretty, slim and perky, with broad, open features and tousled red hair. Her blue gingham dress barely covered the swell of her breasts.

"Hi," she said cheerily. "I'm Cindy McGuire. You come in with Nat Collier, didn't you?"

"Sure did," said Jessie. "I'm Sue Deevers, Cindy. You like a cup of coffee? Be ready in a minute."

"Oh, no—I can't stay long, really." She rolled her eyes and nodded past her shoulder. "They don't much like me wandering off. Just wanted to say hello." She grinned and stuck out her chin. "I'm with Barc Hager's gang. Ever hear of 'em?"

"Well, no, I—" She caught the girl's disappointment and snapped her fingers. "Hey, yeah, I have, too. Sure, the Barc Hager gang."

Cindy's face brightened. "He's comin' in soon with two of the boys. I been here a couple of days, settin' up camp with Red." She made a face and stuck out her tongue. "Barc's pretty nice and the rest ain't bad, but Red's a bastard for sure. God, I hate that man!"

Jessie poured herself coffee and sat back by the fire. "Sure you won't have some?"

Cindy shook her fiery hair. "No, honest, I can't." Suddenly her blue eyes widened, and she bent close to Jessie.

34

"You know who I saw just now, 'fore I come here? William Bonney hisself."

"Really?"

"Honest to God. I swear, Sue." She rattled on, pleased with Jessie's reaction. "Billy the Kid in the flesh. Just walkin' around big as you please. I heard he was ugly as sin, but hell, he isn't bad looking at all. I seen uglier. Damned if I—"

"Cindy, goddamn you!" A deep voice bellowed across the campground and the girl went stiff. "Get your ass back here, and do it quick!"

"Gotta run," Cindy said hastily. "See you later, Sue." A shadow of fear crossed her face as she picked up her skirts and scampered off. Jessie looked up to see an enormous, bare-chested man with legs like tree trunks. Cindy passed him on the run and he swung out with his fist. Cindy shrieked, ducked under the blow, and kept going. The man roared, then stomped off, cursing under his breath.

"Nice folks," Jessie muttered to herself. She figured she'd just met Red, and wondered what he'd do if he caught poor Cindy.

Moments later, Collier walked up and squatted and poured himself coffee. "What's been happening?"

"Just meeting the new neighbors," said Jessie. "You'll like 'em, Nat."

Collier's eyes narrowed, but he ignored the dig. "Told you not to get friendly, remember?"

Jessie's green eyes flashed. "Collier, I haven't left the goddamn fire. What am I supposed to do—shoot anyone who happens to drop by? What's got you in such an itch, anyway? Figured you'd be happy, bein' back among friends."

Collier ignored her and scooped up beans and bacon with his bread. "Got to meet the head honcho," he said, giving Jessie a sour grin. "You'll like her a lot, and she's just dying to meet you."

Jessie stared. *Her?* The boss of this outfit's a woman?"

Collier leered, enjoying Jessie's discomfort. "Sure as hell is. Name's Mattie Lou Lynn. A real charmer, by God."

"You ever heard of her, Nat?"

"Some. She pulled a few scores in California a couple

35

of years back. Know the son of a bitch she runs with better. Name's Cottonmouth Sully. Not much older'n you, but he's got a head of snow-white hair. Real easy-going feller, 'less you cross him. Used to run with King Fisher, if that tells you somethin'. Carries one of them Smith & Wesson Schofields like Jesse James. They say he's fast with it, too."

Jessie frowned in thought. "And this Mattie Lou—she wants to see *me?*"

"Yeah. So eat up fast."

"Why, though? I'm not supposed to be anyone but your woman. Why would she want to see me?"

Collier grinned. "'Cause she saw you ride in, and you're a fine-looking lady."

Jessie swallowed hard. "She—likes women, Nat? Oh, *Christ!*"

"Women, men—hell, probably chickens and goats." Collier laughed and shook his head. "Just take it easy— that ain't why she wants to see you. Not all of it, anyway. She and this Sully keep a pretty tight rein. They want to *know* who's here. You, me, everyone. Period."

"I don't guess I blame them for that."

Collier looked right at her; it was his no-nonsense look, the one that meant he wasn't horsing around. "I don't like the way this business is shaping up, you might as well know it. I got a bad feeling—'specially about Sully being in it. And this Mattie Lou's not right in the head. There's a mean streak in her that's got to come out."

Jessie nodded. She didn't like Collier, but she had to respect him. He'd kept himself alive undercover for two long years, and that said something.

"Somehow *none* of this rings true, you know? I've dealt with the cartel before. They play for high stakes, Nat. People who've bribed, coerced, and murdered their way into high places in this country don't trust their business to folks like Sully and Mattie Lou Lynn. They hire people like that— but someone else runs the show and does the thinking."

Collier shrugged. "I don't know nothin' about that. Captain Simms says you're straight on this cartel business—if he says so, I believe it." He gave Jessie a long and thoughtful look and got to his feet. "You come and set a spell with ol' Cottonmouth and Mattie. Then tell me they ain't rock-solid in charge of this outfit, all right?"

Several canvas tarps had been patched together with leather to form a fair-sized shelter under the trees. At the rear of the place was a crude bar consisting of a couple of planks laid between two barrels. Stumps and empty boxes had been dragged in for chairs. The drinkers looked up when Jessie and Collier walked in. Jessie didn't notice them at all; her eyes were locked on the woman in the corner. She sprawled in an oversized rocker on a straw-mat rug. The rocker was sturdy oak, and needed all its strength against the burden that threatened to overflow its sides.

Jessie silently cursed Collier for letting her walk in cold. Mattie Lou Lynn was more than fat—she weighed three hundred pounds or more. Her thighs were gigantic, her arms bigger around than Jessie's waist. It was her head, though, that made Jessie stare. It was a young girl's head slapped carelessly on a fat lady's shoulders. Hair fell over her face in tight yellow ringlets, framing china eyes and a pixie-red mouth. *Lord God,* Jessie moaned to herself, *what have I got myself into now!*

"Hey, Mattie Lou," grinned Collier, stepping ahead of Jessie, "say hello to Sue Deevers. She's one hell of a gal."

"Hi, Mattie Lou." Jessie forced a grin. "Real glad to meet you."

"Well, well, now..." Mattie heaved her bulk an inch or so higher, and studied Jessie with interest. Bright blue eyes trailed boldly over her body, and Jessie felt a chill at the back of her neck.

"God A'mighty, if she isn't a looker, Nat. Where you been hiding this lady?" The raw whiskey voice seemed to come from somewhere else; it didn't belong to the doll-like face.

Collier slapped Jessie on her bottom. "Me an' Sue's been friends a bunch of years. Caught up with her down in Galveston again."

"Galveston, huh?" Mattie gave Jessie a sleepy smile, but her eyes were hard as stones. "Where'd you work down there, dearie? Miss Morgan's place or the Mansion?"

37

Jessie didn't blink. She was glad now that she'd done her homework on Galveston's numerous brothels.

"I heard about Miss Morgan's, but I don't know the Mansion," she said evenly. "Sure you got the right town?"

"Well, guess I could be wrong," Mattie said smoothly.

"Anyway, I didn't work there or anywhere like it. I don't go in for whorin', and never have."

Mattie grinned, and the men at the bar laughed aloud.

"If you're not a whore, how the hell did you ever meet Collier?"

At this question, Jessie turned and saw the tall, pale-haired man who'd suddenly appeared at her side. She caught Nat's eye and knew the new arrival had to be Cottonmouth Sully. Tossing her hip at a jaunty angle, she looked him straight in the eye.

"Why, hell, if you got to know, mister, I met Nat Collier in church. We was sittin' in the same pew together."

Sully laughed, and Mattie Lou shook all over.

"Perky little thing, ain't she?" said Mattie. "What you think, Sul?"

"Oh, yeah." Cotton winked at Jessie. "Real pretty lady . . ."

Jessie gritted her teeth and glared. She didn't like being discussed like a prize pig at the fair, and didn't care who knew it.

Mattie caught her look and glanced at Collier. "We're *real* glad to have you with us, Nat. Any friend of Dutch's is sure a friend of ours." Her eyes flicked from Jessie to the bar. "You vouch for ol' Nat, don't you, Dutch?"

Jessie turned to see Nat's pale, scarecrow companion standing at his side.

"He's okay by me, Mattie."

Nat Collier flushed. "Hell, Mattie, we got all that business settled!"

"We did, for true," she assured him. "I was just thinking, is all." She looked at Jessie again, her eyes bright with mischief. "Be real friendly, Nat, if you'd—well, you know, kinda let some of the boys here know you're with us. What do you say to that?"

"Shit, I'll buy 'em all a drink, if that'll make you happy."

"I, uh—wasn't exactly thinking about a drink." She

38

grinned, and her eyes flashed at Jessie.

Jessie stared in sudden understanding. "Hey now, just a *damn* minute, lady! I got somethin' to say 'bout—"

"Shut up!" snapped Collier. He stopped her with a look and turned on Mattie. "You bought my gun, lady. You didn't get nothin' else in the bargain."

"What if I say I bought her, too? You feel all that strong about objecting?"

Collier's eyes narrowed. "What are you tryin' to prove, Mattie? Damn, I don't see no one else passin' out free samples."

"You just got here, didn't you? No telling what you might find." Her pale blue eyes flicked to Dutch. "You brought him in. Maybe you'd like to go first."

Dutch leaned easily against the bar and looked at Jessie. "Wouldn't want to dirty Nat's play-pretty."

"Nat doesn't mind all that much. Do you, Nat?"

"Yeah, I *do* mind," Nat said bluntly. "I mind a hell of a lot. I don't see any reason for shit like this. It—well, it ain't right, is what . . ." Jessie saw the bright beads of moisture on his cheeks, the taut flesh at the corners of his mouth. Sully was looking right at him, an easy smile creasing his face. Nat, though, saw something else in the man, something that turned his eyes a color Jessie had never seen. "You got a bad habit of not gettin' girls back in one piece, Dutch—you know?" He forced a laugh and looked sick. "I seen you do it before."

"Nat!" Jessie sucked in a breath and backed away. She stared at Collier, but Collier looked at his boots.

Dutch grinned. "Come on, pretty lady. I ain't going to hurt you. A gal hasn't lived till she'd had old Dutch's brand of loving." He took a step toward her. Jessie stepped aside and her fist came up fast. Dutch grabbed her wrist and squeezed. Jessie gasped at the sudden pain and sank to her knees. Dutch wrenched her to her feet and shoved her roughly toward the door.

Chapter 6

Jessie stumbled and cried out, but Dutch only tightened his grip. She glanced about wildly for help, but knew that not a man in the room would step forward. Every face mirrored Dutch's own pleasure, the hunger in his eyes. If they could take his place, they would. Hell, if Collier was passing the girl around, maybe they'd get a chance at her too . . .

"Just a minute there, friend . . ."

Dutch froze, jerked Jessie around, and forced her to her knees. The man stood six feet away, in Dutch's path. Jessie looked up through her pain and saw a lean figure in a spotless black suit, white shirt, and black string tie. His face was in shadow under a pearl-gray Stetson.

Dutch took the man in, and grinned. "Mister," he said evenly, "I think you're in my way."

"Guess I am," said the man.

"Then move your ass aside. I ain't got the time!"

"I will. Leave the lady alone and it's finished."

Dutch laughed. "Going to have to wait your turn, friend. Now move, 'fore I ruin that fancy suit."

"Dutch . . ." Sully's voice held a warning. "Dutch, leave him alone. I mean it."

"Hell I will," Dutch snarled. *"Move,* you son of a bitch!" In a single motion he tossed Jessie aside and went for his gun. His long fingers moved in a blur; one moment his hand was empty, in the next fraction of a second a Colt was swinging toward the tall man in black.

A single shot roared, filling the lean-to-bar with a flash of white light. Dutch jerked in a circle, stumbled, and fell awkwardly to the ground. The man lowered his weapon, let it hang loosely by his side. Jessie brought herself slowly to her feet. No one in the small shelter moved.

"Damn it, Harrow—" Mattie Lou's whiskey-hoarse voice broke the silence. "I don't want no trouble in this camp!"

The man gave her an easy smile. "Doesn't look like you got any, Mattie." He lifted the flap of his coat and dropped the pistol in its holster, then turned and looked at Jessie. "You feel like getting a little air, miss? Might be you could use it."

"Yes—I'll take you up on that," Jessie said weakly. Without looking back, she brushed herself off and walked out under the trees. The man held back, his gaze touching the others inside before he turned away and joined her.

Neither of them spoke until they were near the edge of the camp by the river. Jessie stopped then, and leaned shakily against a tree.

"Just give me a couple of minutes, will you? Reckon my knees aren't all that steady."

"Yes, of course." He watched her with concern, and for the first time Jessie saw cool slate-colored eyes set in a deeply tanned face. The man's features were well defined, almost sculpted in stone. There was breeding in his look, from the firm line of his nose to the hard plane of his brow. For a moment Jessie was reminded of Roman statues she'd seen while she was in school in Europe.

He caught her staring, and she flushed. With a smile he looked away and walked to the river. When he returned, he offered her his handkerchief, moistened with cool water.

"Here. Maybe this will help. Would you like to sit down?"

"No, I'm all right, really." Jessie ran the wet cloth over her face and handed it back. "Thank you. I'm very grateful. I hope you know that."

He spread the wet handkerchief on a branch, slipped a pencil-thin cigar between his teeth, and lit it with a sulfur match he struck on his thumbnail. "Ah, don't mind, do you?"

"No. Go right ahead."

Blue smoke drifted before his face and he blew it away.

41

He lifted his Stetson and ran a hand through his hair, then centered the hat again. "How'd all that get started back there? If you don't mind me asking."

"No, not at all," said Jessie. "Lord, if anyone's got a right to ask . . ." She stopped then, and gave him a generous smile. "I'm sorry. I heard Mattie Lou say your name, but I don't guess I caught it. Mine's Sue. Sue Deever."

"And I'm John," he told her. "John Harrow."

"Well, John, I—" Her mouth fell open and she stared. "Oh, my God—yes, of *course* you are. John Fielding Harrow!" She shook her head in wonder. "Boy, when I get rescued, I don't mess around! You—" Harrow's smile suddenly faded, and Jessie stopped. "Hey, did I say something wrong?"

"No," Harrow assured her. "My problem, not yours."

"And what problem's that?"

Harrow frowned at the tip of his cigar. "The problem, Sue, is that if you're John Fielding Harrow, you've got to *be* that son of a bitch twenty-four hours a day. Do you understand that at all?"

"Yes, I think I do." She looked quickly over the river.

"Anyway," Harrow went on, "what happened? That fellow someone you know, or just a passing acquaintance?"

"Neither," Jessie said with a shudder. "I came here with Nat Collier. Dutch, the man you—the man you shot, was a friend of Nat's. Mattie thought maybe I ought to"—Jessie looked down at her hands—"uh, get to know some of the boys around camp."

"Oh. I see." Harrow's gray eyes went hard. "That woman's got a bad streak. Liable to do whatever comes into her head."

"You're telling me!"

Harrow studied her a long moment. "Don't guess it's any of my business, but—you don't look to me like you *belong* in this place."

Jessie's heart nearly stopped. Glancing up, she gave him her best Sue Deevers grin. "Might say the same about you, Mr. Harrow. A man with your reputation . . ."

Harrow made a face. "Hell, lady, you *know* what I am. I'm right here where I belong, in this nest of cutthroats and thieves." He scraped his heel in the dirt and glanced back at the camp. "Christ, if the law could build a wall 'round this place, they'd clean up half the West."

Jessie leaned against the tree, twisting one of her unfamiliar braids of dark hair. "You know what I'm saying," she insisted. "These aren't exactly your kind of folks, now are they?"

Any kid with the money for a half-dime novel would know that was so, thought Jessie. John Fielding Harrow was a gunman and a thief, but he was also a gentleman, if his legend was half true, an educated man from a well-to-do family back East. While others ran in a pack, Harrow ran alone. In Denver, he'd held up a whole hotel by himself, emptying the safe and politely asking the ladies for their jewels. In St. Louis, he'd locked a dozen Pinkertons in a vault and walked off with Wells, Fargo gold.

Harrow looked thoughtfully at Jessie, a frown pulling at the corners of his mouth. For a moment she feared she'd asked a question a girl who ran with outlaws wouldn't ask.

"The truth is," he said flatly, "I'm here because of the money. From what I hear, there's going to be a hell of a lot coming. And right now that's something I could use."

Jessie looked surprised. "Lord, what did you do with all you stole? What I always heard it was plenty."

Harrow grinned. "It was. Trouble is, I spent it. On wine, women, and song, as they say. Only I don't recall much singing."

"Yeah," Jessie laughed. "Always wondered about that part myself."

"That's my story. What's yours?"

"Hell," Jessie answered, "I'm just what you see, mister. Whatever shine Miss Deevers ever had, it's all wore off."

"No, that's not true," he told her.

"My father had some money. Not much, but some. Enough to raise three daughters up right. The polish took on two. They got homes and families and men to look after 'em. I was wilder'n a Cheyenne pony from the time I was twelve. They kicked me out of the house the day I hit fourteen."

"Wild *how?*"

43

Jessie gave him a bold and haughty look, bracing her hands on her hips so her breasts stood taut and proud. "With men, Mr. Harrow. What the hell you think? You forget where I was going when you found me?"

A patch of color touched his cheeks. "I'm sorry, I had no business asking."

"Forget it," Jessie said shortly. "Don't matter much, does it?" Then, deciding she'd gone a shade too far, she sighed and took a step toward the river. "Hell, I'm lyin' and you know it. It *does* make a difference, only there's nothing I can do about it now."

"There's always time to change," he told her firmly. "If you want to, that is."

"Oh, yeah? Really?" She turned on him without expression. "Is that what you're going to do, Mr. Harrow? Make a killing here and turn honest?"

"Maybe."

"Sure. And I'm going to cut out and marry a preacher."

Harrow had to laugh. "You'd drive a preacher to drink, Sue Deevers."

"Already did. One or two, at least." She walked away from the river, and Harrow fell in beside her. "You think there's money in this business of Mattie's, huh?"

"I know there is," Harrow said confidently. " 'Course, no one knows just what we're going to steal," he added quickly. "But it's *got* to be big, now doesn't it?"

"Yeah, guess so," Jessie said absently. A sudden chill touched the back of her neck. *He does know, dammit. He won't admit it to me, but he knows!*

Jessie's mind raced. As far back as Galveston, Collier had told her the outlaws were playing it close about the target. No one would know what they were hitting until the last possible moment. Just Mattie Lou, then, and Cottonmouth Sully. Was John Harrow in on it too? He'd let his voice betray him, covered himself too fast.

It makes sense, she thought. *Harrow's a lot more than a holdup artist. He's a planner, a man with a head on his shoulders. There isn't a better man around for maybe the biggest robbery anyone's ever imagined!*

44

Suddenly she saw the good-looking, soft-spoken man beside her in a far different light. Lord, could Harrow be the cartel's inside man? Jessie liked him in spite of what he was, and didn't want to believe it. Still, he was a far better prospect than Mattie Lou Lynn, who was closer to madness than Jessie cared to imagine.

"Hey," said Harrow, "what happened to you? You've been a thousand miles away."

"Yeah, guess maybe I have," said Jessie, "or maybe just *wishin'* I was."

"This, uh—what's his name, Nat Collier?" Harrow said abruptly. "You and him pretty close?"

Jessie's green eyes narrowed. "Why you want to know?"

"I'm just asking, is all."

Harrow's words didn't matter. The look in his eyes had already answered her question. "No," she said carefully, "we're not. I don't guess you'd say we even—*like* each other much. But I'm here with him, yeah."

"Kind of hard to see why, considering."

"John . . ." Jessie wet her lips and laid a hand on his arm. "Look, I like you. I really do. But I can't handle any trouble. Not here."

"Wasn't thinking of causing any."

"I know that, but—"

Jessie's words were lost as a shout went up in the camp. She turned from Harrow and peered curiously through the branches. A crowd was gathering in the clearing past the trees; Harrow took her arm and guided her quickly away from the river. Edging up a small rise, they stopped and looked past the growing circle of men. Jessie sucked in a breath as a familiar figure appeared. It was Red, the bare-chested giant who'd come to chase off Cindy McGuire. He clutched a rawhide whip in one hand, and was dragging someone by the heels with the other. At that instant the crowd closed in around him, and Jessie could see no more.

"What's happening?" she asked. "What's he doing, John? Lord, if that bastard's whipping Cindy . . ."

Harrow edged closer, just as the whip sang and bit into flesh. The crowd roared as leather snaked out once more.

"Fellow's trying to kill some poor damn Chinaman," said Harrow. "Goin' to do it, too, if someone doesn't stop him."

"What!" Jessie's heart stopped. She tore past Harrow, pushing through the crowd. She prayed she was wrong, but she knew already what she'd see . . .

★

Chapter 7

Ki followed the road from the store a good five miles, then turned off into the brush away from the river. Leaving the horse with its load of clanking pots and pans, he moved through the trees on foot. He spotted them near a creek that fed the river. The man named Barc was building himself a smoke. Willy and Hank were readying the horses. Ki nodded to himself, sprinted back to his mount, and started up the road. He was satisfied that the outlaw leader had been serious about the job. It had occurred to Ki that they might just have invited him there to teach him a final lesson, out of sight of the old man and the girl.

When he reached the crossing, they were waiting. The man named Barc nodded curtly at Ki. Hank and Willy pretended he wasn't there. Ki fell in line at a respectful distance to the rear.

Once, while they rested the horses late in the day, Barc turned to Ki and looked him over. "What kinda stuff you cook, anyway?"

"Cook all things you like, sir," grinned Ki. "Beefsteak, chicken. Fine chicken. Nice vegetables too."

Barc made a face. "Forget the vegetables. And I don't want no goddamn chicken, either. Grew up on chicken in Tennessee. What am I supposed to call you? Guess you got a name."

"Chang, sir." Ki bowed from the saddle. "Name is Chang."

"Figures," Barc grunted. "You'll get paid something, Chang. I'll decide *what* when I see how you cook."

Ki hid his surprise at the outlaw encampment. He had to admire the simple scheme—camping out in the open by the river, yet safe from prying eyes. He slumped in the saddle and kept his features in shadow under his hat, letting his eyes touch every face he saw. There was no sign of Jessie or Nat Collier. Of course, that didn't mean they weren't there; the camp was fairly large, spread out among the trees.

Barc pulled up in a tall stand of pecans and gave a shout. A handful of men wandered over to greet the new arrivals. One burly outlaw laughed and tossed a bottle up to Barc. Barc took a slug and threw the bottle to Willy.

Suddenly a shrill cry came from just behind Ki, and he turned to see a young girl race past him. She held out her arms and Barc reached down and swung her up in the saddle and kissed her soundly. Ki caught a flash of red hair and a round, pretty face. Barc playfully grabbed at her breasts and she shrieked and thrashed her feet, giving Ki an eyeful of bare legs and thighs. The men on the ground whistled and hooted, and the girl stuck out her tongue.

"You been good while I was gone?" grinned Barc. He swung out of the saddle and eased to the ground, setting her down beside him. "By God, you better have, Missy McGuire, or I'll damn sure know it!"

Cindy clung to Barc, her eyes flashing angrily at Red. "You keep that son of a bitch offa me," she snapped. "He's been hittin' on me, Barc!"

Red had stepped up to take the horses. Barc looked at him without expression. "That true, Red?"

"Hell, she's been wanderin' off, talkin' to folks," Red muttered. "I just brung her back, is all."

"Yeah, well, you make goddamn *sure* it is," warned Barc. He gave Cindy a slap on her shapely bottom and sent her off. "That there's Chang," he said over his shoulder. "Tell Tommy Blue he's not the cook anymore. Maybe we'll get something decent to eat for a change." He stalked off and left Ki with Red.

Ki took the big man in in a glance—the flat features and mean, squinty eyes spelled trouble, he was already certain of that. If Red dared to push the boss's girl around, it was clear how he'd treat a "chink cook."

"Cookhouse is back there," Red grunted. "There's nine

48

of us eatin', besides you. I want to smell food cookin' in five minutes, and don't burn nothing, either."

Ki was wringing wet by the time he'd cooked up some mush, biscuits, fried dried beef, and boiled coffee. After getting the lean-to and cookshack in order, he hurried to the river with his dirty pots and pans and tin plates. *This is not proper work for a samurai warrior,* he told himself darkly. *I hope Sensei Hirata is not watching from the other world . . .*

He glanced up and peered through the trees. "If you are, master, kindly look the other way," he said aloud.

"Say, you always talk to yourself, fella?"

Ki started and came to his feet. The girl grinned from the bank above, hands stuck jauntily on her hips.

"Ah, I am sorry." Ki lowered his eyes. "I did not know I was not alone."

The girl jumped down beside him and shook her head. "Nothing to be sorry for. I'm Cindy McGuire, and you're Chang, right?"

"Yes. I am most honored to meet you, please."

Cindy tossed back flame-red hair and laughed. "You don't have to do no 'honoring' stuff with me. Here—let me give you a hand. We'll make it back in one trip." She bent to pick up a stack of clean plates, and Ki blocked her way.

"No, it is better I do this alone, yes?"

Cindy gave him a look. "I know what you're thinking, and don't worry. No one around *this* damn place minds if Cindy McGuire carries pots and pans or washes clothes or chops wood. Long as it don't take more'n twenty-six hours a day."

Ki risked a grin and Cindy reached up and pulled off his hat. "Say, you're not a bad-looking man when you ain't all stooped over an' bowin'. Not that it isn't a bad idea, mind you. 'Specially 'round Red. Isn't anything that son of a bitch likes better. Come on, let's get back."

Ki followed the girl up from the river. She walked a few steps ahead, and he enjoyed the chance to watch the firm

49

little bottom twitch under her gown. She was a small girl, shorter and more fully fleshed than the lanky Marcie Brewer. Still, everything was right where it belonged—firm thighs and a waist you could get your hands around, full swollen breasts that threatened to bounce right out of her bodice . . .

Ki caught himself and gave his own rear a swift mental kick. *That's all I need right now—Chang the cook messing around with Barc's woman . . .*

Ki thanked Cindy, stacked the pots and pans where they belonged, and made himself a welcome pot of green tea. Most of Barc's men had wandered off, but Barc himself sat on a log next to the embers of the fire, talking to a man Ki hadn't seen before. He was a sullen looking outlaw in a dusty frock coat and dark trousers. Thick black hair crowned a high, prominent brow and dark-skinned features. A full beard gave the square-set face a longer appearance. The man looked up, saw Ki, and glanced away without interest.

Ki squatted under a tree, well away from the fire. He wondered if he dared take a stroll before dark to look for Jessie, and decided it wouldn't be wise. Not for a Chinese cook. Unless Red sent him on an errand, he had no business away from camp.

Barc and his friend looked up as a newcomer walked out of the trees. Ki studied the man with interest. He was young, still under thirty, but his hair and eyebrows were white as snow. Barc stood and smiled, but his friend didn't move.

"Hello, Sully," said Barc. "Come and sit and have some bad coffee or a drink."

Sully shook his head. "Can't. Got a bunch of shit to do for Mattie. Listen, there's a meeting on the hill up past the river. 'Bout eight. Be there, Barc, it's real important."

"Well, I sure will. What's it all about?"

Sully grinned through his teeth. "Tell you when you get there, all right?"

Barc nodded and stepped back from the fire. "I guess you know Clay here, don't you? He just rode in and we was catching up on old times. Him and me go all the way back to Tennessee together."

Sully nodded. "I know Mr. Allison by reputation," he said evenly. "Pleased to have you with us."

The dark-bearded man looked up and let his eyes touch Sully's. Then he looked back at his boots and said nothing.

Sully peered narrowly at Barc. "Understand you brought a chink cook into camp."

"Yeah, I got me a cook."

Ki sat up straight as Sully's pale eyes sought him out. "You bring hands in that we don't know, you're supposed to tell me or Mattie."

"Shit, he's just a cook," Barc said flatly. "He ain't no *hand*."

"Just do it, Barc, all right? Makes things easier all around." He glanced at Ki once more, then turned and stalked off.

Allison followed Sully with his eyes. "Real pisser, isn't he?"

"Yeah, he's all right," Barc growled. He spat on the fire and reached in his vest for makings, and started to roll a smoke. "Got a burr up his ass is all."

Allison looked past him. "Let me tell you about a fellow like that. Got a fast hand, good eyes, and guts—and none of that's worth shit in a fight if you get the drop on him first. Don't let him spook you, friend."

"Come on," Barc protested, "he doesn't bother me a bit."

Allison almost smiled. "Yeah, well, I wouldn't let a man talk to me like that. I surely wouldn't, Barc . . ."

Ki stood and worked his way casually back to the cookshack. Even before he recognized the name, he knew Clay Allison was a man to be avoided. He saw him with his eyes, but he also knew him with *kime*, the samurai sense that has no name. The image of a serpent came instantly to mind—dark, cold, and cunning. Ki was certain that everything he'd heard about this famous killer was true.

He stayed in the cookshack, rattling pans and doing work that didn't need doing. It would be dark soon, and he added a few sticks to the fire and made fresh coffee. Let them see him working, get used to having him around. It wouldn't take long before no one bothered to notice where he was.

Ki wondered if he dared try to get close to the meeting that the man named Sully had mentioned. What else could it be about besides the outlaws' target—information he and Jessie desperately needed? He decided he almost had to take

51

the chance, though it was much too soon to start wandering about. If Red came looking, he'd say he'd been relieving himself by the river. What could anyone say to that? Even Chinese cooks had to take care of their business...

—"Chang? What on earth are you doing? I thought you were all finished!"

Ki turned to see Cindy McGuire just behind him. A wisp of tawny red hair fell over her eyes and she blew it back in place.

"Cleaning up some," Ki told her. "Want to do good job."

"Well, you don't have to work all night. They'll get plenty out of you, believe me." She glanced about the shed and looked pleased. "You sure got everything neatened up fast. That goddamn Tommy Blue was a pig—had the place in such a mess you couldn't find nothin'. Oh—if you don't mind me saying so, be best if you set that sack of flour in the barrel with the meal." She stepped up quickly on a box to lift the sack off its makeshift shelf. "We get a little rain and it'd wet this down for sure. One time I—aw, *shit!*"

Too late, Ki saw the box split and collapse. Cindy lost her balance and fell flat on her back. The flour went flying, the sack bursting like a bomb on the floor.

"You are all right?" Ki said anxiously. "You are not hurt?" He bent to help her and Cindy waved him off.

"Just broke my ass is all," she said shortly. "Hell's fire, if that wasn't a damn fool thing t—" She stopped abruptly and her eyes went wide. Ki looked over her shoulder and saw Red towering above them, a dark scowl spreading across his features.

"D-don't you touch me, Red!" Cindy backed off fearfully across the floor. "You do, an' I'll tell Barc for sure!"

Red hesitated, glared at the girl, then turned and jerked Ki to his feet.

"No!" Cindy protested. "Leave him alone, now. He didn't do a damn thing!"

"Right," Red replied with a nasty grin, "but *he* ain't screwin' the boss, now is he?" He tossed Ki back to the ground, grabbed his leg, and started hauling him out of the shed. Ki protested loudly, crying out in fear and yelling the few Chinese words he could remember. With his free hand,

Red reached into the crook of a tree, snatched up a rawhide whip, and kept going.

Ki's mind raced. In a moment he'd have to decide. Taking a second beating in less than twenty-four hours didn't appeal to him at all. He could maim or kill the big ox in a hundred different ways, but then what? He wouldn't be the docile Chinese cook—no one would mistake him for that. An ounce of lead between the eyes would put a sudden end to his disguise.

Red stopped in the clearing, reached down, and ripped Ki's shirt off his back. Ki scrambled on his knees across the dirt. The leather struck his back, sending a sharp jolt of pain through his body. Ki yelled, and didn't have to fake it. The whip came down again and he rolled aside, letting the leather sting the ground. Red cursed and kicked him in the belly. Ki gritted his teeth and covered his stomach. Out of the corner of his eye he saw a crowd gathering to watch. The whip sang again, this time catching his shoulder and flailing his chest.

All right, he told himself grimly, *that's about enough, friend* . . .

Springing to his feet, he turned and faced Red in a crouch. The big man looked surprised and came at him, the whip trailing easily on the ground. Ki watched his legs, and knew what was coming. Another step, then the whip would come at him from the right and take him at the waist. Before that happened, Ki would be inside the man's reach. His feet would lash out and break the wrist that held the weapon; stiffened fingers would drive for the throat in the quick *shuto-uchi,* the knife-hand strike . . .

Red moved. Ki started for him and, in the small part of a second, changed his mind. The whip came at him, and Ki ducked. Nothing was there to counter the motion, and Red followed through with the blow, stumbling to keep his feet. A man in the crowd laughed, and then another. Red stalked Ki across the clearing, his face flushed with anger. Ki kept dodging and darting about, careful to keep a frightened look on his face. The whip snapped dirt at his heels. Ki threw up his arms and ran. Red bellowed and popped air an inch from Ki's rear. He howled and leaped in the air,

53

pretending the blow had struck home.

Ki now had Red doing exactly what he wanted, chasing him in a circle. The crowd was roaring with laughter. A whipping and maybe a killing had turned into a circus; the outlaws were pleased with the diversion, and didn't much care how it ended.

Suddenly the laughter stopped and Ki risked a glance over his shoulder. Red wasn't running; he was cutting across the circle, determined to finish off his prey. Ki had nowhere to go. The men weren't about to let him past and spoil the show.

I will have to fight him. There is nothing else now. If I have to kill him, I'm dead. And if I don't—

Barc Hager stalked into the clearing with Cindy on his heels. "Christ, Red, leave the chink alone," he said sourly. "You're actin' like a goddamn fool." He jerked the whip from Red and turned on Ki. "Get that yellow ass of yours back where it belongs," he bellowed, "or I'll take this whip to you myself!"

Chapter 8

Jessie sat on her blanket against a tree, well away from the fire. The sun was gone, but the earth held on to its heat. If the night cooled at all, she knew it wouldn't happen till three or four in the morning.

Green flies buzzed about her plate and she swept them aside. The ham and bread were good, but she was too nervous to eat. Lord, Ki was right here in camp—and of all the rotten luck, he'd run into Cindy's tormenter!

Jessie stood and stretched, her thoughts turning again to John Harrow. His reaction to her concern for the "Chinese cook" told her a lot. Whatever he might be, Harrow was a cut above the others. He'd understood her anger at seeing a man get whipped. Rawhide against bare flesh wasn't his kind of fight.

Nat Collier showed up a moment later, and Jessie knew he'd had more than a few slugs of whiskey.

"Understand your friend's in camp," he said shortly. "Got hisself whipped, did he?" Collier squatted by the fire and scooped food onto a plate. Jessie noted that he still hadn't looked her in the eye.

"You know anything about a man named Barc? That's who Ki's with. I met his girl this afternoon."

"Heard of him," Collier grunted. "Works out of New Mexico Territory and Colorado, mostly."

"One of his boys, the one called Red, is the fellow who whipped Ki."

"Uh-huh."

"I've got to figure some way to contact him. Cindy's all right, but of course I can't say anything to her."

Collier looked up and blinked, a shred of ham poking out of his mouth. "Hell, woman, you can't say nothin' to *any*one in this place. I hope you got that straight."

Jessie's eyes flared. "Oh, I got it *straight,* Collier. I'm sure as hell learning who I can and can't trust!"

"Aw, shit." Collier looked pained. "Just what'd you expect me to do, huh?"

"How about something real simple, like, 'I'm not passing my woman around, Mattie, and that's that.'"

"Sounds real simple. It ain't, and you know it."

"What I know, Collier, is that you let that crazy fat lady bluff you. She doesn't pull that stuff on everyone who walks into camp."

"You know that, do you?"

"I know you backed down and let Dutch take me out of that bar! My God, Nat, he *killed* that poor Mexican girl when he got through using her. If Harrow hadn't shown up—"

Collier blurted out a laugh. "You listening to yourself, woman? You hear what you're saying? Christ, we ain't been here a day and you got everyone all sized up. Dutch and his boys are *bad* outlaws, right? And John Fielding Harrow's a saint. Damn, that bastard's no better'n the rest. Be a good idea if you kept that straight."

Jessie turned away so he couldn't read her expression.

"Anyway," Collier went on, "I haven't got time to worry 'bout Harrow or you or the Jap or anything else. There's a meetin' tonight. Sully's asked a bunch of us to be there."

Jessie sat up straight, all her anger forgotten. "Nat, it got to be a planning meeting, doesn't it? Maybe they'll tell you the target. If they do—"

"If they do, they're out of their goddamn minds," he said flatly. "Cottonmouth and Mattie've got more sense than that."

"You're right," Jessie said reluctantly. "Still, if we know what kind of a job it is, that'll help."

Collier looked at her and grinned. "Shit, I ain't worried. When the right time comes, you just rub those fine pointy tits of yours up against Harrow. He'll tell you the goddamn target and sing 'Dixie' all at once."

"Damn you," Jessie flared. "Collier, you are a—a—Oh, *hell!*"

Collier turned and walked away and left her fuming. It didn't help at all that she'd been thinking about Harrow in exactly the way he'd guessed. She liked the man, and couldn't help her feelings. The idea of getting close to Harrow stirred old familiar urges—urges that had nothing at all to do with who or what he was...

There were plenty of men about, but no one bothered her as she walked from one fire to another toward Barc Hager's camp. *It's a perfectly reasonable thing,* she told herself soberly, *one woman visiting another. There's nothing suspicious in that. At least I can let Ki see me, let him know I'm here, even if we can't get together.*

Cindy welcomed her warmly, as if they were long-lost friends. Jessie couldn't help but like the young woman. It was clear that Cindy had never known any life but the one she had, and didn't imagine she could hope for anything better. Still, no matter how life had abused her, it hadn't broken her spirit.

"Let me get you a cup of coffee," the girl said eagerly. She giggled and guided Jessie away from Barc Hager's fire, past the bedrolls and tents. "I'd offer you somethin' stronger, but Barc keeps the good stuff hidden. He can't abide a woman who drinks."

"I got loose as quick as I could," Jessie told her. "I was worried about you, Cindy. That big ape didn't hurt you, did he?"

"Red? Naw, he has to *catch* me first. And I know better'n to let him do that. Besides," she added proudly, "I told Barc as soon as he got in, and he told Red to keep his hands off me or he'd get what-for!"

Jessie walked about slowly, glancing at every face she saw.

"I, uh—saw that business this afternoon. That was Red whipping the Chinese fellow, wasn't it?"

"Oh, hell, yes it was," Cindy said darkly. "I put a stop to that, though. Made Barc call him off. Chang didn't do a damn thing. It was just Red's meanness—he was getting even with me."

"I hope the poor man wasn't hurt."

Cindy shook her head. "Red didn't get him good but twice. He's over takin' it easy in the cookshack." She stopped then, and peered curiously at Jessie. "You mind if I ask something personal? You do, just stop me and I'll shut my big mouth."

Jessie laid a hand on her arm. "Cindy, ask me anything you like."

"What—what's it like, talking to a feller like John Fielding Harrow?" Her eyes got wide and she shook her head in wonder. "Lord God, Sue, I'd wet my britches for sure if that man just *looked* in my direction! What'd he say to you? Did he—you know—*touch* you or anything? Damn—he wouldn't have to shoot no one for me, I'll tell you. He could have me just for the asking."

Jessie tried to hide her smile. Obviously the outlaw camp was like a very small town. Whatever stories there were got around fast. "He's a real nice man," she said solemnly. "All we did was walk down to the river and talk."

"That's all?" Cindy's face fell. She came close and leaned into Jessie. "You'd tell *me*, wouldn't you? I mean, it won't go no further."

"Promise. If there was anything to tell."

Cindy seemed satisfied with that. She walked beside Jessie, chattering about what she'd seen in camp, and what a girl named Bethann Parker had done with a dozen men down at the river. Finally Jessie said goodbye, making sure the walk ended five yards from the cookshack itself. If Ki was nearby, she was certain he'd heard her voice.

Walking through the encampment, she kept to the center of the path, as close to the firelit clearings as she could. It was getting on toward ten, she decided. Collier might be back from the meeting, with news. Of course, it would be blind luck if they learned the cartel's plans this soon; Collier was right about that, but it didn't hurt to hope. The sooner they had some answers, the sooner she and Ki could—

Jessie heard the noise in the trees—a dry twig snapped underfoot, cloth whipped against a branch. She quickened her steps and kept going, forcing herself not to break into a run.

Just keep walking . . . the next fire's right ahead and you can make it . . .

Suddenly the man was standing directly in her path. Jessie sucked in a breath, spun around, and ran. The second man was waiting. She came up hard against him and he crushed her roughly to him. Jessie tried to scream, but a hand covered her mouth. Branches stung her cheeks as they dragged her quickly back through the trees. The land sloped down and she sensed they were taking her toward the river. The man who held her stopped, tossed her roughly to the ground, and pinned her arms. She could see him now, and the others. There were three of them. One squatted down by her face, so close that she could smell his sour breath. The other stood above her, his hands on his hips. The pale light of the moon touched his features, and Jessie knew the face at once. It was the towheaded youth she'd seen on the trail. *Lord God, it's them—Dutch's boys, all three of 'em!*

The boy saw her expression and grinned. "Real pleased you remember," he said softly. "That's going to make it more fun. We figure you *owe* us, girl."

"I don't owe you a damn thing!" Jessie blurted. "You and your—"

The man went to his knees and slapped her hard. Jessie gasped and tears stung her eyes.

"What you think now, pretty? Huh? You goin' to make this easy or what?"

"Shit," growled the man holding her arms, "let's quit talkin' and get at it, Josh. I'm stiffer'n a damn board!"

The man with the bad breath giggled. He reached over and squeezed Jessie's breast. Jessie bit her lip in pain and jerked her head away.

"All right," said Josh, "peel those trousers down, Burt. I'm goin' to dip my rod in that sweet little hive and get me some honey."

"Not afore I do," the other complained. "Hell, I'm already on her and I'm goin' first!"

"Do it, then," Josh said harshly, "and don't take all night about it."

"I don't aim to," Burt replied huskily, and began tearing at Jessie's belt and the buttons of her denims. He gripped

59

the waist of the trousers and stripped them down over her hips. "Lord," he breathed as the silken nest between her thighs came into view, "if that ain't the prettiest little—"

He stopped in puzzlement as something fell from the trousers onto the ground beside Jessie's hips. Lowering his head to peer more closely at it in the dim light, he saw that it was a double-barreled derringer with ivory grips. "Josh!" he exclaimed. "Looky here what I done found. Why, it's a damned old—"

Suddenly Burt's weight was removed from Jessie as he rose off her, straight into the air, and disappeared. Josh clawed for his pistol as something dark came at him in a blur. A fist lashed out and his head snapped back and he fell to the dirt in a heap. The third man sprang to his feet and ran, bellowing at the top of his lungs. A hand grabbed his collar and turned him around in midair. There was a sound of snapping bone, and the man's eyes bulged and a torrent of blood gushed from his mouth and nose as he collapsed like an empty sack.

Jessie stood quickly, buckled up her denims, and replaced the derringer in its former hiding place behind her belt buckle. She was shaking like a leaf. A shadow came toward her, then stopped suddenly and vanished as voices called out and lanterns bobbed among the trees. Cottonmouth Sully burst through the brush, his Schofield pistol in hand, holding his lantern high.

"You all right? What in hell's been—" He took a step toward her and his light touched the two twisted figures. "Christ, what's going on here, girl?" He bent to inspect the two men, then looked up and caught her eye. "I don't figure you did this, so who did?"

Jessie shook her head. "I don't know. But whoever the hell it was, I'm glad he came."

Sully let out a breath. "One of 'em is dead already. The other's not far from it."

"Cotton, there's another one back here," one of the men called out. "Deader'n shit, too. God A'mighty, someone broke every bone in his face!"

"And you didn't see a damn thing, right?"

Jessie's green eyes flashed. "Look, mister, those three

60

bastards pulled me off in the trees, and I don't have to tell you what for. I don't give a damn *who* stopped em. I wish to hell I did so I could shake the man's hand!"

Sully looked her over, then burst out laughing. "Lady, I reckon I'm going to have to chain you up, 'fore that pretty little ass of yours flat runs me out of hands!"

Chapter 9

Collier didn't return until well after midnight. Jessie pretended to be asleep, though it was clear he was stumbling about purposely, trying to wake her. She was up at dawn, making coffee and frying salt bacon, when he sat up and scratched and stomped over to the fire.

"Understand you had another big evening," he growled. "Christ, woman—"

"Oh, yeah, real big night," Jessie said lightly. "Nothing I like better'n a good gang rape before I turn in."

"You got away, didn't you?"

Jessie looked at him. "I'm such a whiner, you know? Always making something out of nothing."

"All right, all right . . ." He held up his hands in surrender. "Don't guess I can blame you for bein' upset. Who was it killed Dutch's boys? Cotton said you didn't know. That the truth?"

"Of course it's the truth. Like I told Sully, I don't much care." She split a cold biscuit and stuffed it with hot bacon. Collier waited to see if she'd serve his plate. When she didn't, he let out a breath in disgust and jammed a biscuit in his mouth.

"You going to tell me about the meeting?" Jessie said finally. "Or do I have to ask?"

Collier shrugged. "Not that much to tell. Told you there wouldn't be, didn't I? There was *two* meetings. The one I was at was for all the gang leaders. Not that I got any goddamn gang, 'cept you."

"Nat, get to it," Jessie sighed.

"What they did mostly was run through what we're goin' to be doin'. Who does what, and all that. We're all headin'

62

out to the flats in the next couple of days to *practice*."
Collier made a face. "Can you believe that? They got this
dummy town staked out. Strings and sticks for buildings,
that kinda stuff."

"Well, at least we know it's a town now, don't we? That
lets out trains."

"Maybe. I'm not sure yet that they're tellin' it straight."

"Why not? Anything this big, Collier, it's got to go
smoothly. They can't very well keep you in the dark."

Collier set down his coffee. "No, but they can sure throw
us off, keep everybody guessing. They've already started
on that. They got us divided in seven troops, all right? Just
like the army. And after last night, we won't be meetin'
together again. You see what that does, don't you? You
learn your part, but you don't know shit 'bout what anyone
else is doing. Mattie Lou made that real clear. Anyone
talking about his job to a feller from another troop . . ."
Collier showed his teeth and ran a finger across his throat.

"Yeah, I see what you mean," said Jessie. "Doesn't make
our job any easier, does it?"

Collier grunted. "Hell, it makes it damn near impossible,
is what it does. All I'm gettin' is a little piece of the puzzle."

"You said there was another meeting," she prompted.
"What was that about?"

"Likely everything *we* want to know," Collier muttered.
"Sully ran that end of the show—took four or five fellers
up the river to talk. Your friend John Harrow and Doc
Holliday—I don't know who else."

"Holliday's here?"

"Yeah, he's here." Collier looked amused. "Him and
Harrow's old running buddies. Surprised you didn't know."

"I just met Harrow yesterday," Jessie said stiffly. "He
hasn't gotten around to his life story, Nat."

"Uh-huh. 'Spect he will, though."

"Now look, damn it!" Jessie flared.

"Hey, hold on," Collier said blandly. "I got no objection
to you playin' house with John Harrow. I'm plumb *countin'*
on it, lady. He knows where this bunch is going to hit. *I*
sure as hell don't."

"And you think he's dumb enough to tell me, right?"

63

Collier gave her a look that made Jessie blush all over. "By God, darlin', *I* sure would."

Jessie gathered up her pots and pans and tin plates and walked to the river. Several people were already there, and she picked a spot well away from the others. The blazing Texas sun had warmed the rocky bank, and the air was thick and sultry. Jessie decided that if she didn't get a good bath soon, she'd start to smell like Collier. From the moment she'd met the man, it was clear he avoided soap and water like poison.

Bending to her task, she filled the bean pot with water to let it soak, then started scrubbing plates with river sand. In a moment she heard footsteps on the path, glanced up casually, and went back to her chores. He picked a spot six feet away and started scouring a large skillet with a rag.

"Use some sand in that and it'll be a lot easier," Jessie said without looking up. "Going to take you all day like that."

"Thanks," Ki said gruffly. "That's all I need right now, more good advice."

Jessie held back a grin. "Thought maybe you'd figure this was a good place to meet. Lord, Ki—thanks for showing up when you did last night! If you hadn't been there . . ."

"I followed, after I heard you talking to Cindy," he explained. "Thought we could get together then, after you left. I heard the men talking in camp this morning. The ones who attacked you—two are dead, are they not?"

"Yes, they are, Ki." She caught the tone of his voice, and risked a look in his direction. "You did what you had to do. You know what they had in mind for me."

"I regret killing, Jessie. Even if it has to be done. Now tell me. Have you and Collier learned anything at all?"

"Some, but not a whole lot." She quickly told Ki about the meeting Collier had attended, and the one Cottonmouth Sully had held for a privileged few.

Ki nodded. "I know about the meetings. Barc Hager's friend, Clay Allison, is here. He attended the meeting with this Harrow and the others. Hager was angry, because Allison wouldn't tell him a thing."

Jessie shuddered. "Lord, I've heard about Allison. How

64

many men is he supposed to have murdered?"

"Whatever the number, I believe it," said Ki. "Be careful, Jessie. As I told you from the start, I don't like you counting on Collier. He's already shown how much you can trust him."

"Oh, you heard about that, huh?"

"Collier backing down from this Dutch? Yes, Jessie. Everyone in camp has heard it." He gathered his pots and pans and stood.

"You be careful too," Jessie warned. "Don't push this Chinese cook business too far."

"It is a very good disguise," he said evenly. "I can assure you no one will see through it."

"I've *eaten* your cooking, Ki. Okay?"

Ki muttered something under his breath, and stomped away from the river toward the camp.

Ki quickly learned that the life of a camp cook left little time for anything else. Even though he was cooking for ten at the most, he barely had time to clean up one meal before it was time to start the next. After the noonday feed, he carried his pots to the river, then hurried back to peel a small mountain of potatoes. He had to admit Jessie was right; he was not well suited to the fine art of cooking. Red had promised to flay his hide and make him fry it if he burned the biscuits again.

It was nearly two when he finished the potatoes and started on a stew. The meat was longhorn beef and as tough as leather. Ki finally carried it out to a stump to chop it with an ax. Halfway across the clearing, Clay Allison stepped up and blocked his way. He looked at the haunch of meat in Ki's hand and sniffed.

"That's supper, is it?"

"Yes, sir," Ki replied, ducking his head subserviently. "Make fine stew. Very good meat."

"It stinks, you dumb son of a bitch." Allison's coalblack eyes looked right through him. "I don't want any goddamn stew. You understand that? You cook me some fish, boy. A nice fat river catfish." He tapped out the last few words on Ki's chest.

Ki blinked. "You want fish?"

"What the shit did I say?"

"Yes, sir. Mr. Barc—he say stew tonight. Chang no have any fish."

Allison raised a brow. "Then *get* some, hear?"

Barc Hager came through the trees with Cindy McGuire, saw the pair, and stopped. "What's going on, Clay? Chang here challenge you to a draw?"

Allison wasn't amused. "Just arranging supper, friend. Your cook's going to catch me a nice fish."

"Yeah, well..." Barc looked down at his boots. "Fine, if that's what you want."

Allison glanced at Cindy. "You run along with the Chinaman, girl. Make damn sure he comes back." The outlaw walked off, and Barc turned and grabbed Ki by the collar. "Look, I got enough goddamn problems as it is," he said harshly. "You get that son of a bitch a fish, boy. Come back without one, and I swear to God I'll give you to Red!"

Ki welcomed the chance to leave camp, especially wtih Cindy McGuire. He had no idea how the stew would get fixed in time for supper, and didn't much care at the moment. Clearly, Hager was scared to death of his old friend. Allison wanted a catfish, so the rest of the crew could starve.

"Listen, you ever catch a fish before?" asked Cindy. "I don't know a damn thing about it, and don't much want to, either."

"Oh, yes," Ki said eagerly. "Catch plenty good fish."

"Bullshit," Cindy said darkly. "You'd say 'oh, yes,' no matter what, Chang."

Ki gave her a narrow look. "Miss Cindy—is not good idea for Chinese person to say *no,* eh? Get in plenty big trouble."

"Yeah, suppose you're right about that." She swept red hair off her shoulders and kicked at a rock with her boot. "You know what, Chang? You and me are 'bout the same notch on the pole. A goddamn Chink and a woman. Long as we're useful, we don't get whipped."

Ki didn't answer. Judging from what he'd seen, the girl had every reason to feel the way she did.

A mile upriver he found a spot he liked. The shallows

gave way to deep water as the river made a sharp bend to the west. Past the bend was a tangle of logs and brush. A big oak grew on the bank, its roots spilling into the water. The logjam had formed a small inlet, masking the spot from the rest of the river.

"Fish here," Ki said. "Very good spot."

Cindy gave the place a dubious look. "Good spot for moccasins, you ask me."

Ki walked a few yards up the bank, cut a stout pole, and attached the line and hook he'd borrowed from one of Barc's men. Making a floater from a piece of dry wood, he baited the hook with a chunk of meat he'd taken from the shed. Cindy watched him curiously as he lowered the line carefully into the water.

"That's it? The fish grabs on to that, huh?"

"Yes. If we are lucky."

"He isn't going to go for that beef," she said solemnly. "What you need's some really stinkin' chicken. A catfish'd eat that up."

Ki looked at her. "Excuse me. Chang thought you knew nothing about fishing."

"I don't. But I keep my ears open, you know? My pa used to say that all the time."

"Yes. He was right," Ki agreed. "But we do not have chicken, do we?" He squatted on the bank and watched his bobber intently. It twitched once, then stopped.

"What was that, a fish?"

"Only a very small one."

"How you know that?"

"Wood not move much. Fish not big."

"Oh, yeah." Cindy stood up and yawned. "Look, Chang—this fishing is so goddamn excitin' I can't stand it. I'm going around the bend and take me a bath. You get through with this shit, come and get me."

"Yes, I—" Ki's mouth suddenly went dry. Cindy undid the buttons of her blue cotton shirt, stripped it off her shoulders, and let it fall. A pair of firm, milk-white breasts sprang free. The lovely globes were tipped with dusty rose, dimpled by the sudden touch of a breeze. Cindy leaned against a tree to unbuckle her denims, slipped them off her legs, and

67

stepped free. Twisting on the balls of her feet, she gave Ki a saucy grin.

"Catch a real big fish now, hear?" she said brightly. "You need anything, I'll be 'round the trees." Turning, she pranced off up the bank. Ki caught a quick glimpse of flame colored fur between her thighs. The sight was quickly replaced by an enticing view of a firmly rounded bottom and willow-slender legs.

He followed her with his eyes until she was gone, then turned his gaze on the unmoving bobber in the water. "Bite, you little bastard," he muttered aloud. "I'm not waiting around for you all day."

Chapter 10

Ki left the bank and walked up the slight rise into the trees. From the rise he could see upriver, and back the way they'd come from the outlaw encampment. A few nearly invisible wisps of smoke rose up from the forest.

"Good," he said darkly. "Maybe Red's cooking my stew."

Leaving the rise, he made his way down to the river. Green willows arched over the water, masking a small pool. Cindy floated on her back with her eyes slightly closed, her hair spilling like liquid fire over her shoulders and breasts. Ki stopped and let out a breath, feeling his loins stir at the sight. Errant shafts of afternoon sun pierced the willows, patterning the girl's flesh with coins of light. The light turned the color of her skin to cream and honey. Beads of moisture danced on the tips of her breasts and jeweled the feathery nest between her legs. Ki took a step forward, and Cindy opened her eyes and grinned.

"Hey there! Catch any fish?"

"Yes. Two very small. One big."

Cindy looked relieved. "Good. Ought to make that scary bastard happy. You feel like a bath? I heard somewhere that Chinamen take baths all the time. Either them or the Japanese. Can't remember which."

"I think it is both," Ki said soberly. "Oriental people very clean."

"Well then, hop on in." Cindy laughed and came to her feet. Cupping her hands, she sent a spray of water toward the bank. The motion set her upturned breasts to dancing, a rhythm that caught Ki's eyes and held them.

"Uh, yes, I—think I will," he said, the words as dry as sand in his mouth. Without taking his eyes off the girl, he slipped off his loose cotton shirt and stepped out of his trousers. Somewhere in the back of his mind were several reasons why this was anything but a good idea, but Ki ignored them all and stepped off the bank into the river.

Cindy let her eyes trail boldly over his body. She bit her tongue and stared as her gaze came to rest on his groin. "Lord A'mighty, Chang—look what you been hiding! Way you prance around, bowing and scrapin', I figured maybe you was a walkin' bowl of mush." She shook her head in delight. "Boy, was I ever wrong!"

Ki waded to her, stopping a foot away. Cindy's blue eyes were wide, her lips slightly open.

"You—really do look different," she said softly. Ki caught a touch of hesitation in her voice, a slight spark of fear in her eyes. "You're just not the same man at all."

Ki gave her a foolish grin to put her at ease. "Oh, yes. Chang same person."

"No. No, you're not..." She brought one hand out of the water and laid it carefully on his shoulder. Her eyes bored intently into his. She let her fingers trail over his chest, then drew them away as if she'd touched a hot stove. "My God," she said in wonder, "you're as hard as iron all over. Just as lean and strong as a—as a wolf or something!" She gave him a long, curious look. "Who are you, Chang? Honest? And don't tell me you got a body like that from cookin' bad biscuits."

Ki had to smile. "Not always cook. Work on ranch sometimes. Do much, much hard work and—"

Cindy pressed a finger to his lips. "You're lying, and I expect you've got good 'reason." She wrapped her arms around his neck and drew him to her. His shaft brushed her belly and she sucked in a breath and closed her eyes. Ki slipped his arm about her back and kissed her open mouth. Cindy shuddered and made a tiny noise in her throat. His tongue explored the sweet, warm hollows of her mouth. She answered with a hunger of her own, her sharp little tongue darting frantically past his lips. Ki stroked her back, letting his hands slide over the sleek wet flesh to the slender curve of her waist. She pressed her body against him, moaning with the pleasure of his touch. Her breasts were hot

70

points of fire against his chest. She was shorter than Ki, the top of her tousled head coming only to his chin. She stood on the tips of her toes, straining to reach him, stretching her arms to grasp his shoulders.

Ki knew what she wanted. His hands found the delicious curve of her bottom and lifted her up to meet him. Cindy gave a joyous little cry and scissored her long legs about him.

Arching her back, she linked her fingers behind his neck and leaned lazily toward the water. Her breasts were proud peaks of beauty under his gaze; he watched bright droplets of water sparkle the hard points of her nipples. She let go with her arms and let his grip hold her, trailing her hands limply in the water. Ki drew her gently to him until the underside of his member stroked the firm crest of her pleasure. Cindy sighed, the hollow of her belly rising and falling with his touch. He pulled her hard against him, released her, then drew her closer still. She caught the rhythm of his hands and ground herself against him, moving the flesh between her legs in a slow, easy circle of delight. Ki felt the pressure of her legs against his back, the ever-increasing tension in her thighs. Cindy's breath came in short little gasps. He watched the skin grow taut about her mouth, saw the cordlike muscles strain against the soft flesh of her throat. He released her then, slipped her legs from their grip, and raised her in his arms. Carrying her out of the water, he laid her gently on a soft patch of grass on the bank. She gazed up at him, her pale blue eyes smoldering.

"Oh, Lord," she moaned, "you—just about got me there, you know? I'm—hanging right on the edge."

"Yes," he whispered, "I know."

Ki marveled at the firm swell of her breasts, the tight, pouty nipples tipped a dusky pink. He cupped one of the lovely mounds in his hand, squeezing it gently to bring the water-kissed bud into his mouth.

"Ahhhh, yes, *yes!*" Cindy trembled as he drew the hard points between his lips. Her breasts slid easily under his touch, until pliant flesh filled his mouth. The heady scent of musk assailed his senses. One of Cindy's hands came up to slide under his own. Her strong fingers eagerly kneaded

71

her breast, forcing it even farther into his mouth.

Ki felt her other hand snake past his belly and seize his erection. At first she circled his shaft gently, teasing the length with the soft tips of her fingers. As his tongue drew the swell of her breast ever deeper into his mouth, her hand moved faster, sliding the loose skin over firmer flesh beneath.

"Please!" she whispered, her words hot explosions against his throat. "Stick it inside me now—I need you—way deep inside me!"

Ki's own hunger was surging within his loins, and he needed no further invitation. He moved between her thighs, and her long legs opened to welcome him in. Cindy groaned, and when his hand cupped the soft nest of her pleasure, she opened her mouth wide and laughed with joy. His fingers spread moist petals aside, revealing a kiss of rosy flesh. He stroked the silken mound, letting his fingers trail gently into the sweet, honeyed warmth below.

"I—can't take that," she pleaded. "I'm—I'm too hot to wait—honest!"

Ki didn't answer. His fingers moved lazily up her cleft until they rested against the shell-pink crown. At his touch, Cindy's whole body shuddered. Her back arched in a bow, jerking up to meet him. Ki moved his fingers in a circle, watching the little nubbin swell and grow. He slid his hands beneath her hips and lifted her onto his thighs. He entered her slowly, letting his shaft glide easily into her warmth. Cindy gave a lazy sigh of pleasure. Her arms clung to his back and drew him to her, as her hips thrust up to meet him. Her mouth went slack in a smile, and her eyes looked longingly into his.

"Yes—like that. Keep coming—*real* deep—oh, yeah, right there!"

Again he leaned over her breasts and took a nipple into his mouth. She thrust her belly against him, straining to draw him in farther. Her hands pressed hard against his back, then slid down to grasp his hips. Velvet muscles between her thighs tightened around him, heightening his desire. He thrust himself rapidly against her, so hard that the motion forced the air from her lungs. A ragged animal cry began deep within her throat. Her slender form trembled beneath him. She shook her head wildly from side to side, whipping his face with her fiery hair.

Ki felt his own release building, climbing to a delicious peak of pleasure. Cindy sensed his need and pounded his back with her legs. Her sharp cries were muffled against his shoulder. She grasped his hips with her nails and squeezed hard. Ki cried out and emptied himself inside her. Cindy screamed, her face a mask of pain and pleasure. Her silken warmth spasmed, tightening again and again around his member. He was empty, drained, but Cindy refused to let him go. Ki gasped in surprise as the familiar pressure filled his loins again, then exploded with a surge even greater than before. Cindy laughed with joy, gave a final sigh, and collapsed in his arms.

"Oh, Lordy," she whispered, her eyes filled with wonder. "You are some kind of a man, Chang. I never imagined I'd be—" She stopped then, lowered her eyes quickly, and turned away.

"What's wrong?" Ki asked. "What is it?" He reached down and turned her face toward him.

"I, uh—got a little confession to make, is all." She bit her lip contritely and let out a breath. "Truth is, I didn't expect anything like this. Damn, not that I'm complaining!"

"And what *did* you expect?" Ki asked coolly. "You stood right there and stripped off your clothes. What did you think I'd do?"

"Nothing," Cindy said dryly. "That's just it." She looked up and held his eyes. "I was—*teasing* you, is what I was doing. I'm not real proud to admit it, but it's true."

"You were—" Ki suddenly understood. A quick flush of anger rose to his cheeks and he gripped her shoulders hard. "Yes. Of course. The Chinaman's not truly a man. It's all right for a girl to show him her body."

"No, you—yes, goddamn it, that's it," she said harshly. "That's exactly what I was thinking. Do you hate me for that?"

"No, I don't. You didn't understand."

"Listen, you." She reached up and pulled him back down and kissed him soundly. "I ain't askin' to get off the hook.

73

I'm a fool and I deserve a kick in the ass. Just because I didn't know better's no excuse. I hurt you, and I didn't mean it. You believe that, don't you?"

Ki looked at her, saw the glint of tears in her eyes, and wiped them away. "Yes, Cindy, I do. It's all right."

Cindy sniffed, blinked to clear her eyes. Suddenly her full lips curled in an impish smile. "Cindy, now, is it? What happened to 'Oh, yes, Miss Cindy. I catch plenty good fish.'"

Ki laughed at her painfully accurate imitation. "After what happened just now, I don't think I can handle the 'Chinese cook' business with you."

"Good. 'Cause I can't handle it either." Her expression suddenly went sober. He caught the alarm in her eyes, the tension in her body, and knew she'd remembered who they were and what they were doing. "I knew it," she said cautiously, "when I saw your body, the strength there, and the way you looked at me."

"What do you want to know?" he asked evenly. "Who I am? Why I'm pretending to be something I'm not?" He shrugged and gave her a smile. "It's not that big a mystery. I'm not Chinese—I'm half Japanese and half American. And I act the way I do because that's how people expect me to act. I had a good job in San Francisco. I got in a fight with a white man and killed him. It wasn't my fault, but that doesn't matter. If I'd stayed they'd have hung me straight off." He grinned and tousled her hair. "And I *am* a cook, really. Or sort of one, at least. I worked a couple of ranches in the Panhandle, then drifted down here. I needed work, and Barc Hager hired me."

"Yeah, well, that explains a lot." She looked up and smiled. "Thanks. Thanks for trusting me."

He felt the tension drain from her body and knew she believed him. He'd sensed she wouldn't betray him, but now he was certain.

"Is that your real name? Chang?"

"No, it's not. But if it's the only one you know, you won't have to remember what to call me."

"Yeah, guess you're right about that." She thought for a moment and gave him a studied frown. "And you really did catch some fish? That's the truth, ain't it? 'Cause if it's not, we're in a hell of a lot of—"

"No, that's the truth. I wouldn't want to face Clay Allison without a 'very nice catfish. Plenty good, sir...'"

Cindy clamped a hand over her mouth and giggled. Then the smile suddenly faded and she sat up in alarm. "Lord, what time you figure it is? If Red or Barc or one of those bastards was to come out looking... I don't even want to *think* about that."

"No," Ki said soberly. "Barc Hager's woman lying naked with the Chinese cook. Not a real pretty picture."

"Hey now, don't you dare say that." She stuck out her chin and frowned. "I think it's one hell of a fine picture. And, Lord, it sure did *feel* real fine!"

Their eyes met for a moment, and Ki felt a stirring inside him again. A tumble of red hair fell over his face. Her deep blue eyes were glazed with sudden hunger. The full, sensuous mouth was half open, and Ki could see the pink tip of her tongue between her teeth.

"Hey," she said hoarsely, "we've got to go, remember? And that isn't what I want to do at all. Damn, I can feel it startin' up. I'm gettin' all wet again."

"Where?" said Ki. "You mean *there?*"

"Yes, I mean—ahhh!" She sucked in a breath and feebly slapped him away. "Yes, right there!"

"Then you are right," he said solemnly. "You are definitely wet again, Cindy."

Ki sat at her waist, his hand resting gently between her thighs. Cindy drew herself up on her arms, her eyes fixed dreamily on his hands, unable to move from under his touch. As he stroked the lush mound below her belly, her mouth opened wide and went slack. Her head fell back, revealing the slim column of her throat. Ki let his eyes feast on the naked stretch of her legs, the delicious hollow that swept from the flat of her belly to the curve of her ribs. She was a small and lovely creature. As the sun warmed her flesh, it brought forth a heady, tingling perfume that brought Ki to the height of arousal. Spreading her thighs with his hands, he slid down the length of her body to lie between her strong, shapely legs, his mouth hovering at the portal of her sex

75

like a honeybee above a pearly pink flower. Lowering his head, he began to kiss the sleek petals, touching them lightly with the tip of his tongue.

Cindy trembled and went rigid. A startled cry escaped her lips and her belly jerked up to meet him. She sat up quickly, staring at him with wonder.

"Wha-what on *earth* are you doing, Chang? Lord, I never felt anything like that!"

He reached a hand up and gently pressed her down. She sprang back up as if her body were on a spring. "Damn," she said shakily, "I mean that, mister. I really never did!"

"A man has never kissed you there before?"

Cindy shook her head. "Not ever. I *heard* of it, of course, but it sure never happened to me. It's—all right, ain't it? I mean, to pleasure me like that?"

"It's perfectly all right." He smiled. "And very enjoyable too. As you'll see, if you ever stop bouncing around."

"Gawd, mister, you do that and I'm sure as hell not lyin' still. That's the most—ooooh, yes, *yes!*"

Ki slid his tongue lightly over the slick folds of flesh. Cindy's whole body shook. He caressed the lovely hollow, thrusting his tongue ever deeper inside her. Again and again Ki tasted the honeyed joys. Cindy's slender form seemed to sing as he lifted her closer and closer toward a release she'd never known. She clawed the earth with her fingers, arching her back until her bottom twitched off the ground. Ki thrust his tongue deeper and deeper until he felt the creamy flesh begin to spasm. Quickly he withdrew his tongue and clamped the hard and swollen pearl between his lips.

Cindy gave a long, unearthly cry of joy. Her body jerked uncontrollably, then fell back limply to the ground. Ki moved up beside her and took her in his arms. Cindy clung to him, covering his face with desperate kisses. Tears filled her eyes and scalded Ki's cheeks.

"Oh, Lord," she cried, "I don't know who you are or where you came from, Chang, and I don't much care. You're the only man who *ever* showed me any real loving. You know that? You ain't hurt me or called me names or treated me like dirt. You just give me everything that's fine, and no one *ever* done that before." She held his cheeks between her hands and looked fiercely into his eyes. "I belong to you now, whether you want me or not. I ain't ever lettin' you out of my sight!"

My God, Ki thought, appalled at what he was hearing. *Now what have I done?*

Chapter 11

A pair of enterprising outlaws had rightly guessed that their companions would miss the finer things of life after a day or two by the river. They'd come to the gathering with a flatbed wagon piled with goods, which they now proceeded to sell at outrageous prices. There were cigars, tinned peaches, sacks of flour and meal, potatoes and onions, a barrel of apples, and sacked hams. Everything but liquor, Jessie noted. The drinking trade in camp belonged strictly to Mattie Lou Lynn and Cottonmouth Sully, and no one tried to compete.

Jessie bought one of the last of the hams and some onions, and started back down the path. John Harrow spotted her there and smiled and touched his Stetson and motioned her over. He was standing next to a gaunt, almost cadaverous-looking man in a rumpled black suit and a white shirt open at the collar.

"Morning, Sue," Harrow said politely. "Don't think you've met John Holliday, have you? Doc, allow me to introduce Miss Deevers."

Jessie blinked with genuine surprise. "Lord, you *are* him, aren't you?"

Holliday gave her a weary smile. "I am afraid so, ma'am, and there's little I can do about it, it seems."

Jessie blushed and shook her head. "I'm sorry, I didn't mean *anything* like that."

Holliday took off his hat, pulled a linen handkerchief from his pocket, and mopped his brow. His dark hair and mustache seemed darker still against almost ashen skin. "You, my dear, may say anything you like," he said firmly. "May I tell you, you are the loveliest lady I have ever had

78

the pleasure to meet? That's not too forward, I hope?"

"No, I—" Jessie felt her cheeks color again, and touched a hand to her throat. "Why, thank you very much, sir."

Harrow grinned and squeezed Holliday's shoulder. "He's right, of course. You're all of that, Sue. But I'd advise you not to listen to this fellow too close. Doc's an expert in three fields of endeavor: dentistry, charming the ladies, and cheating at Spanish monte."

"Nonsense," Doc snorted, "a man with a keen mind and a steady hand doesn't *have* to cheat at cards." He fastened his eyes on Jessie. "I've been trying to persuade friend Harrow to abandon this foolishness and join me in Tombstone. There's profit to be made there, and I assure you the food is better at the Maison Dorée." Holliday twisted his mouth in distaste. "Lord, how could it possibly be anything else?"

"Too rough a town for me," said Harrow. "You and me together, we'd likely get in a hell of a lot of trouble."

"I'd be willing to put that in writing," Holliday said somberly. He nodded politely at Jessie. "If you'll excuse me, miss. It has indeed been a pleasure." Placing his hat back on his head, he turned and walked up the path toward Mattie's makeshift saloon.

"Doc's an old friend," said Harrow. "We go way back." He pulled a cigarillo out of his pocket, then changed his mind and put it back. He looked at Jessie with concern. "I heard about last night. Are you all right, Sue?"

Jessie shrugged and walked along with him, carrying her sack. "Yeah, I'm all right. I got a little help before things got rough." She cocked her head and gave him a playful look. "Thought maybe it was you that came to my rescue. Wasn't, though, was it?"

"No," Harrow said evenly, "I'm afraid not. I saw those two before they buried 'em. Whoever it was, he plays rough. Don't think I ever saw a man killed like that."

She caught the hint of a question in his eyes, and pretended not to notice. "To tell you the truth, whoever it was pure scared the hell out of me, John."

He stopped on the path and caught her eye. "I—don't guess I understand."

"Well, you would, if you'd been me," she said bluntly. She looked right at him, trying to make the words real. "That son of a bitch wasn't doing me any favor. He killed Dutch's boys so he could have me for himself. I *know* that, John. I could feel it!"

Harrow studied her a moment, "Christ, Sue, if that's true, we've got a madman running loose!"

"Well, that sure does amaze me now, you know? In a fine place like this?"

Harrow had to laugh. "I'm sorry. Hell, you've got a good point." He laid a hand gently on the small of her back, and Jessie didn't protest. Neither spoke for a long moment, and after a while Jessie saw that they'd wandered past the encampment and found the river again. Harrow lit his smoke and glanced out over the water.

"What do you figure on doing?" Jessie asked him. "After this, I mean."

"Seems like we talked on this before," said Harrow. "What I'm doing, lady, is retiring. If the take's what it's supposed to be, I'm finished for good. What about you? You staying with this Collier fellow?"

Jessie didn't miss the way he made the name sound like a curse. "Don't know," she said absently. "Might or might not."

He faced her then, his eyes suddenly dark. "I can't see that, Sue. Not for you."

"And just how *do* you see me, Mr. Harrow? You going to take me to St. Louis, or maybe New York City? Buy me a trunkful of gowns and take me to nice places?"

"Yeah. I might just do that."

Jessie laughed. "Oh, sure!"

Harrow took two quick steps, pulled her into his arms, and kissed her soundly. It was a fierce, bruising kiss, full of both anger and passion. Jessie fought him, then yielded, opening her lips to welcome him in. When he finally let her go, she gasped for breath and backed away.

"My God, John—"

"I've been wanting to do that," he said shortly. "I'm damned if I'll apologize for it."

"And who asked you to? You might—take it a little easy next time, though."

"And when's the next time going to be?"

"Whenever you want it to be," Jessie said quickly, not even surprised at her answer. *Lord, what am I doing?* she thought. *John Harrow's likely the man I came to get—and not on a blanket, either!*

Harrow's mouth twisted in a wicked grin. "Well, the next time can't be too soon for me. I guess you know that."

"Yeah, I guess I do," said Jessie, the words sticking in her throat. She tossed her braids off her shoulders and gave him a challenging grin. "Maybe I'll just buy those fancy gowns myself," she teased. "Might be I don't need me a John Fielding Harrow. Is this business *really* all that big?"

"Big enough," Harrow said evenly.

"How big? You were at the head men's meeting, weren't you?"

"Who told you that?"

"No one." Jessie shrugged. "I don't know—everybody's talking about who got invited and who didn't."

"Then everybody talks too goddamn much," he said coldly. "Come on, I'll walk you back to camp..."

Just before supper, Nat Collier announced that Mattie Lou and Sully were throwing a party at their makeshift saloon.

"Tomorrow morning we get down to work," he said. "I reckon that's what we're supposed to be celebrating."

"Fine," said Jessie. "You have a good time. If you don't mind, I'll pass on Mattie Lou's party."

Collier's flat features went hard. He reached out and squeezed Jessie's arm until she winced. "Damn you, lady, I *do* mind!" he said harshly. "What the hell you think I brung you for, anyway? You knew this wasn't no Sunday social 'fore we started!"

"I'm doing my part," she said coolly. "You told me to hang around John Harrow. That's exactly what I'm doing."

"Oh, yeah?" Collier gave her a baleful eye. "Bet that chore makes you sick, don't it?" He caught her look and burst out laughing. "Shit, you play the part better'n I figured. You make a damn good outlaw's whore!"

"That's enough now!" Jessie's green eyes blazed.

"Forget it," Collier said flatly. "You're going, and that's that."

There were close to two hundred men in the encampment; the party was much too big for the lean-to saloon, which was now closed off behind a plank-and-barrel bar. Every lantern in camp hung from the trees, and makeshift tables had been set up for gambling and drinking. Someone had brought out a fiddle, and couples were dancing in a circle on the hard-beaten ground. Jessie guessed there weren't more than two dozen women in camp, and they were all popular tonight, regardless of their looks.

After a moment she spotted Cindy McGuire standing with Barc Hager and some of his men. Jessie wanted to talk, but decided to wait for a better time. The girl looked miserable and more than a little scared. More than likely, Jessie guessed, Red was bothering her again. Damn the man anyway, she thought, suddenly angry at Cindy's lot. Why did Barc Hager let the big ox treat her that way? Most of the time he didn't seem to care.

Collier came up beside her and gripped her arm, his breath smelling of whiskey. "Come on," he told her, "move around and talk to folks. Don't want 'em to think we're unfriendly, do you?"

"Oh, hell no," Jessie said flatly. "I don't want that."

Collier gave her a chilling look and edged her forward. She spotted Harrow and Doc Holliday playing cards with three other men. Harrow looked up and Jessie returned the smile.

"There's Cottonmouth and Mattie Lou," said Collier. "We better say hello. They'll expect it."

Jessie tried to dig in her heels, but Collier had her firmly by the arm. Mattie looked up and spotted Jessie, her eyes sparkling with pleasure.

"My, honey, you look simply *lovely* tonight," she purred. "I do declare you do." She wet the tip of her tongue and glanced boldly at Jessie's breasts. "Ain't she a delight, Sully?"

"Evening, Miss Deevers." Sully half closed his eyes and glanced at Collier. "How are you, Nat?"

"Fine party," Collier blurted. "By God, it surely is something, I gotta say that!"

Jessie shot him a look, wishing he'd keep his mouth shut. She did her best to keep from staring at the pair. Sully looked grand in an elegant pearl-gray frock coat, a new Stetson, and a fresh ruffled shirt. Mattie Lou looked like a clown. Her face was heavily powdered, and two puffy ribbons crowned her head. She wore a bright yellow gown laced with frills, which only served to accentuate Mattie Lou's incongruously doll-like appearance.

"Whyn't you sit and talk a spell?" said Mattie Lou. She patted a space on the barrel next to her massive personal chair. "We ain't had time to get acquainted, now have we?"

My God, thought Jessie, *the woman's out of her mind. Does she think I've forgotten what happened right here, and who brought it about?*

"No," said Jessie, "we haven't. I don't think we're going to, either." She looked at Mattie Lou and didn't move. For a moment, anger touched Mattie's cheeks, and her china-blue eyes went cold. An instant later the little-girl smile was back, as if nothing at all had happened.

"Well, now. Sully dear, why don't you get Mattie Lou another drink? My throat's dry as dirt." Sully nodded and moved off toward the bar. Mattie looked straight at Collier. "Your little lady here ain't learned how to behave, Nat. I'm real disappointed. I figure you ought to teach her better."

Collier cleared his throat. "Damn it, Mattie—hasn't there been enough trouble?"

Mattie Lou heaved her great bulk forward. "Collier, I *do* want Sue and me to have a little talk. Now you want that too, don't you?"

Suddenly Collier's face went hard. "No, damn it, I don't want her to do any such thing, lady. I'm doing *my* job here, and that's all you got to worry about. That clear enough?"

Before Mattie Lou could speak, Collier grabbed Jessie roughly and pulled her away.

"My God," Jessie said breathlessly, "she never stops, does she?"

"That woman's plain sick in the head is what she is," Collier said angrily. "Hell, she's got it in her mind to have you, and she ain't goin' to leave me alone till she does. Well, it ain't going to be, and that's the end of that. You are right. I never should've brung you here tonight."

Jessie looked at him. "Nat, thank you. Really."

"Hell, woman . . ." He made a noise in his throat. "Don't go thanking me for something I didn't do. 'Cause it isn't you, it's me. I'm tired of taking her dirt, is all."

"I thank you just the same."

"To hell with your thanks," Collier said bluntly. "I don't need 'em." He turned on his heel and left her, stomping away toward the bar.

Jessie let out a breath. She was no drinker, but she decided she could use one herself. Clawing through the crowd, though, wasn't worth the effort, and she walked back outside under the trees. Cindy McGuire saw her and rushed to her side.

"God, isn't she just *awful?*" She rolled her eyes back to the bar. "I swear, that woman scares me more'n Red does. Well, damn near, anyway."

"Yeah, she's a caution," Jessie agreed. She studied Cindy a moment. "What in the world's going on with you, anyway? A couple of minutes ago you looked like you'd lost your last friend. Now you're the cat licking cream."

Cindy blushed and stared at the ground. "Guess I was thinkin' on something real nice, is all. Lord, if I told you, you'd just die." She glanced cautiously over her shoulder, then brought her lips close to Jessie's ear. "I met this man, Sue. I mean, it was the last thing I ever expected to happen—"

"Cindy, wait—" The crowd around them had suddenly gone silent. Dancers stopped and gamblers looked up from their cards. Jessie stared past Cindy, straight into Nat Collier's eyes. He stood with his back pressed against the bar. His face was pale. Clay Allison stood before him, hands hooked carefully in his belt. He leaned slightly forward, spoke to Nat, and grinned. Jessie couldn't hear the words, but the stricken look on Collier's face spoke eloquently.

Allison turned to the crowd and shook his head in wonder. "Feller here insulted me. Just flat out called me a liar."

"I didn't do any such damn thing," Collier protested. "What the hell you pushing me for, mister!"

"I'll be damned." Allison looked pained. "He went and did it again."

"Look, now—"

Allison casually spat in Collier's face. Collier's features clouded with rage, and Jessie saw his hand move shakily toward his weapon.

"Go on," Allison urged. "Do it, mister."

Collier hesitated, made a fist, and dropped it to his side.

"Well, shit." Allison looked disappointed. Without warning he reached under his coat and drew his revolver, thumbed back the hammer, and fired it directly in Nat Collier's face. A sharp explosion brightened the night. Collier's features vanished. The side of his skull blew away, splattering the canvas wall, and he slumped limply to the floor.

Allison jammed his revolver back in his belt. When he turned, his eyes darted through the crowd and found Jessie. "Let's go," he said softly. "I think Miss Mattie wants to talk to you, girl."

Jessie shrank back in horror. An arm reached out and shoved her roughly aside. Jessie started as John Harrow stepped in her path.

"Mister, I don't want any trouble. But you can have it if you want it."

Allison's eyes narrowed. His gaze flicked from Harrow to Jessie's right. Doc Holliday leaned casually against a tree, pulling at the end of his mustache.

Clay Allison glared. "I don't think this is any of your affair, Harrow, now is it?"

"Yes, sir, it is," Harrow said evenly.

"His too?"

"You'll have to ask Doc about that. I don't speak for him."

Allison nodded and searched Holliday's eyes.

"There's no reason for ill will between us," said Harrow. "All we got to do is call it off now."

For an instant Allison's eyes raged with fury. A muscle twitched in his jaw, and his hand moved imperceptibly at his side. Then his features relaxed and he nodded at Harrow. "We'll talk again sometime, mister."

"As you like," said Harrow. He stood perfectly still, not moving at all until Allison walked off through the trees. Jessie let out a breath and tried to stop shaking. The shooting had soured the party, and the crowd began to thin; a small group stood around Collier's body, discussing who would take charge of the burial.

"Might be a good idea if you and me took a walk," said Harrow. He touched Jessie's face and looked in her eyes. "You all right now?"

"Yes, I'm—I'm fine." She glanced past Harrow to the bar. By now, someone had tossed Collier's coat up over his face. Two men were squatting by his side, going through his pockets and laying the items up on his chest.

Chapter 12

An hour after sunup, half the outlaws had already left for "maneuvers." Barc Hager's gang wasn't slated to leave before noon, but Ki already had more chores to do than he could possibly finish. Red wanted everything packed and ready to go: camp supplies, tents, horse gear, and the contents of Ki's cookshack. Ki explained patiently that he couldn't break down the shack yet. His explanation brought an angry cuff to the head, and the promise of worse if he didn't comply.

Swallowing his fury, Ki waited until Jessie passed his camp, then grabbed an armload of pots and followed her to the river. Stopping a few yards away, he began scrubbing a crusted kettle with great vigor.

"My Lord, Ki," said Jessie, "I can't tell you how glad I am to see you! You know about Nat, don't you?"

"I didn't trust the man, but I'm sorry," he said quietly. "He didn't deserve that."

"He was trying to help me. He wouldn't admit it, but he was. I got him killed, Ki."

"No," Ki said flatly. He peered at her from under his frayed hat. "That's not true and you know it. Mattie Lou got him killed, not you."

"Yeah, well, my being here sure helped."

"He was undercover two years, Jessie. I think it was starting to wear thin. You said so yourself. Look—Barc's as nervous as a cat, doing everything he can to avoid Clay Allison. Allison's hitting the bottle and looking for trouble. The word is no one ever backed him down before. He doesn't much like it."

87

"John Harrow said the same thing," Jessie sighed, "but he doesn't seem worried. Ki, Mattie Lou put Allison up to that, and Allison killed Nat just for the *fun* of it. He didn't even know him!"

"You're staying with Harrow now?"

"Yes, I am. He's all right—I'll be just fine." She knew she'd answered too fast, that Ki could read the strain in her words. "He's very nice, really. I know what he is, damn it, but he's not like the others." She paused, then risked a look in Ki's direction. "The way he acts has got me kind of confused. I know he could be the cartel's man. He's certainly the logical choice. Still..."

Ki thought for a moment. "Do you have any way of finding out for sure?"

"No. Not yet. We're going out with Troop Two for a couple of days. Same bunch as yours. Maybe I'll come up with something. We've *got* to, Ki. With Nat gone, it's all up to us. And we don't have much time left."

"Uh-oh," muttered Ki, "here comes Red. I've got to get moving. Be careful, Jessie."

Jessie started to answer, but Red bellowed a curse and Ki scampered off.

She sat on the side of the hill and watched the four flatbed wagons rattle down the road. The wagons were covered with canvas, drawn by two horses each. The covers bulged as if they contained a heavy load—sacks of grain or corn in neat piles. Jessie had watched the run-through a dozen times before, and knew the loads were fakes. When the wagons reached the staked-off squares of the "town," the canvas would fall away and armed men would spill from each wagon and run to their posts—"buildings" on either side of the road. Seconds later, other outlaws would tip the four wagons on their sides to block both ends of the street. The instant the positions were secure, seventy-five riders would lope down the road and race through an aisle between the wagons, every other man holding the reins of an extra mount, or those of a packhorse draped with leather bags. Half the riders would mill about, intently sweeping imaginary windows with their weapons. The others would pour

88

into the "buildings," then emerge with make-believe loads to be packed hurriedly on the horses. An instant later, everyone in the street would be mounted up and gone.

Jessie stretched, and wiped her bandana across her brow. The action told her something, but not nearly enough. What town were they raiding, and what were they after? There were too many parts of the puzzle that simply didn't fit. Fewer than half of the outlaws were practicing here on the flats. What were the others doing? What was their part in the plan?

Three riders pulled up in the trees just below. She recognized Harrow at once, and Sully and one of his riders. The sight of Harrow stirred a familiar warmth, and a flush of color rose to her face. *Damn it all, you've got no room for thoughts like that—not with John Fielding Harrow!*

Sully and his man rode off. Harrow glanced up the hill, caught her eye, and waved. Jessie waved back. Then Harrow wheeled his mount around and trotted off. That was *all* he'd done the last few days—waved and ridden off. For some reason she couldn't fathom, he'd kept his distance since she'd come to stay in his camp. Jessie was both relieved and disappointed. He certainly hadn't shied away from her down by the river. What was bothering him now?

Barc Hager's new camp was close to Harrow's. Jessie could wander over whenever she liked, with the excuse of visiting Cindy. She usually saw Ki, but there was never a chance to get near him. Red was riding him hard, watching him like a hawk. He'd even started following him to the creek to watch him wash pots.

"I swear to God," Cindy said tightly, "that man's got the devil in him, Sue. He's going to kill poor Chang, and likely me too, 'fore it's over!"

"Cindy," Jessie said crossly, "why does Barc let him treat you like that? I can't understand it."

Cindy bit her lip to keep from crying. "'Cause it gives him pleasure, that's why. There's something in Barc that's not right. I—I've seen it coming a long time." Jessie read the plain, naked fear in the girl's eyes. "I think he *wants* Red to take me," she blurted. "I think it—excites him to think about that!"

At this revelation, Jessie's belly knotted up, and she felt a sudden urge to turn and run...

Harrow had somehow bargained for slabs of tender beef, and Jessie fried them. They wolfed down the steaks with relish, and Jessie couldn't remember when anything had tasted quite so good.

"I'm not even going to ask where you got them," she moaned, leaning back on her blanket. "I don't much care, I'm just glad you did."

Harrow grinned, the first time she'd really seen him smile in some time. "You wouldn't believe me if I told you."

"Try me."

"The steaks you just enjoyed were a present," he said absently, "from Frank and Jesse James."

"Huh?" Jessie sat up and stared.

"True. They really were here. They just wouldn't get close to the encampment. Sully wanted me to talk 'em into staying."

"And did you?"

"Nope. Didn't figure I could. Everywhere's too hot for those boys. Don't much blame them. Mattie's mad enough to spit nails. Says it makes it look bad for everyone else, if the deal's not sweet enough for the James boys—you know?" Harrow squinted into the fire and shook his head. "Sully says Billy the Kid's gone too. Back to New Mexico Territory. I'm not even sure he was ever here. Except maybe in Mattie Lou's head."

"You don't think so? I've talked to a couple of people who've seen him."

Harrow grinned. "Hell, I can do better than that. I've shaken hands with *three* William Bonneys. One of 'em was close to sixty years old!"

Jessie laughed, and began to clear away their plates. "I wish Clay Allison would leave," she said soberly. "We could do without him."

"He's still around. Sticking close to himself."

"You be careful, John. Really."

He held her eye a moment. "You worried about me?"

"Well, of course I am," Jessie said sharply. "Does that surprise you?"

"No, I—thanks, Sue."

Jessie sat up on her knees. "Hey, is anything wrong? Did I do something to get crossways with you?"

"No, of course not." Jessie caught the slight edge to his voice.

"Well, she said dryly, "I sure am glad to hear that."

"Look, dammit!" He stopped then, and the sudden anger faded. "I'm sorry. I've got a lot on my mind. This business is getting close."

Jessie looked at her hands. "How close?"

"Day after tomorrow." He glanced up quickly and frowned. "And keep that to yourself. No one's supposed to know till tomorrow night."

Jessie's throat was suddenly dry. "Yeah, right," she told him. "I won't breathe a word."

From the slow shifting of the stars, she guessed it was well after one. Harrow slept soundly across the dead fire, but his silence didn't deceive her. A man like that would come instantly awake at the slightest sound that didn't belong. Taking a deep breath, she peeled the blanket aside, came to her knees, and crawled carefully toward the brush. She took her time, testing the ground every inch until she was a good ten yards into the trees. Finally she came to her feet and stood quietly in the dark. Her body shook all over, and she took deep breaths the way Ki had taught her.

I wish to hell you were with me, she thought. *You're a lot better at this kind of thing than I am.*

She shrugged the thought aside and moved away. Ki *wasn't* there, and that was that. She'd have to try it herself, and it had to be tonight. If she couldn't learn the truth now, there wouldn't be another chance.

The waist-high ravine ran through the camp, east of the spot where they'd set up the makeshift town. Someone had shot two rattlers there the first day out, and everyone had avoided the place since then. Crawling out of the depression, she crouched on her haunches and waited. Cottonmouth

91

Sully had a tent of his own, a good twenty feet from Mattie Lou's. Going to her hands and knees again, she edged up close to Mattie's tent and listened. Mattie snored soundly. Jessie crawled a few feet farther on and peered cautiously through a slit in the canvas. The woman was an enormous mound of flesh on the far side of the tent. A kerosene lamp hung from a pole, the wick turned low. Jessie let her eyes move slowly around the shelter, carefully noting everything she saw. There were two wooden chests against the wall. One was shut, the other flung open and overflowing with voluminous dresses. There was a wooden table, two kegs, and Mattie's oversized chair. Nothing was on the table except a half-empty bottle.

Jessie's heart sank. The enormity of what she was doing suddenly hit her. Her chances of finding what she wanted were next to nothing. Maybe Sully had it and not Mattie. She hadn't dared try Harrow; the few personal belongings he carried were always on him. Maybe they were all playing it close, not writing anything down . . .

Jessie gritted her teeth and moved cautiously into the tent. The open trunk seemed a thousand miles away. She knelt down beside it and ran her hands carefully through the clothing. Nothing. No envelopes or wallets where she might hide papers. With a glance at Mattie Lou, Jessie eased up the lid of the other trunk. In the dim light of the lantern she could see it was filled with silken garments—petticoats, shifts, pantaloons, and a tangle of items she couldn't begin to identify. All were sewn with silk and velvet ribbon and edged with delicate lace—each garment large enough to fit a fair-sized mare.

Beneath the frothy clothing were several bundles of stiff-backed photograph cards tied with ribbon. The cards were stamped *Belles de Paris*. Jessie glanced at several pictures, and saw all she needed to see. One showed a dozen naked girls squeezed into the scene, twisted in nearly impossible positions. Another pictured very young boys.

Jessie carefully closed the lid. Once more she let her gaze wander about the tent. *Nothing, nothing.* Suddenly something caught her attention that she hadn't seen before. It was the edge of a leather case, peeking from under the

blanket by Mattie's head. Jessie's heart leaped. Of course—
that had to be it! Mattie would keep anything that important
close to her all the time.

Taking a deep breath, she crawled from the trunk to
Mattie's blanket. The obese woman was turned to face the
wall of the tent; the fact did little to diminish her looming
presence. Jessie was close enough to touch the tight blonde
ringlets, smell the sharp edge of strong perfume. The great
hulk heaved under the blanket, rising and falling in rhythm
with deep, resonant snores.

Jessie reached under the blanket and carefully eased the
case from the weight of Mattie's shoulder. The slim packet
slid into view and came free. Unfolding the case, she eased
the sheaf of papers onto the blanket and turned the first
sheet over. Jessie could have cried out with joy. The paper
was a map, plainly showing the main encampment on the
Nueces River, and a dotted line leading north. There were
other trails and streams, and marks she couldn't understand,
but Jessie paid them no heed. Her eyes were locked on the
name of the town, printed in bold black letters at the end
of the dotted line. Lord God, talk about gall—the cartel's
target was the capital city of Texas!

Jessie's mind raced. What was the outlaw's objective?
A bank? Wells, Fargo? She realized it didn't much matter.
All she had to do was get word to the Rangers. Once they
knew the target was Austin, they'd bait their trap and wait,
then draw it up tight with the outlaws boxed inside.

Jessie carefully replaced the map on top of the sheaf and
peered at the next. It was a long list of supplies: rifles,
ammunition, extra wheels and harnesses for wagons. Jessie
blinked at one item. The outlaws had enough dynamite to
blow up half the state! She lifted the paper and peered at
the next. Another list, she thought impatiently, and turned
the next sheet. It was a map, almost like the first. Maybe
it—

Suddenly, Mattie Lou heaved a great sigh and rolled in
Jessie's direction. Jessie froze in horror, then jerked back
from the descending mountain of fat. Mattie's shoulder
caught her hand holding the papers and crushed it to the
ground. An arm the size of Jessie's waist hit her solidly in

the neck. Jessie stared, too frightened to move. Blonde ringlets brushed her cheek. Mattie Lou's sleeping face was only inches from her own...

Chapter 13

Jessie didn't dare breathe.

Mattie's swollen features filled her vision. Her mouth sagged open, heavy lips bubbling in sleep. Jessie nearly gagged from the stench of her breath.

If she opens her eyes, wakes for even a second...

She counted pores in the bloated face, traced the thin line of hair above the lips. Slowly she started inching her hand from under the woman's shoulder. Mattie snorted and her eyelids fluttered. Jessie went rigid, willing herself to relax, to stop her heart from pounding. She could never get free on her own. Mattie would have to do it for her, roll away and free her hand and lift the massive arm off her neck.

Jessie's left arm was flattened, but her right was still free. Carefully she groped around behind her, running her fingers blindly over the bedding and the bare earth beyond. There was nothing, only dirt and small stones. *What I need right now's a big fat bug to stick in her ear,* she thought grimly. *That, and a good half-mile head start...*

Suddenly her fingers closed on something soft. Jessie tested it in her fingers, and knew it was one of Mattie's voluminous garments, draping over the edge of the trunk. She tugged it lightly and felt it slip free. Slowly she bundled the cloth together. She knew exactly what she had to do next, and the idea scared her out of her wits. If it didn't work...

To hell with it. It was risky, but no more so than lying there all night, waiting for Mattie to wake up.

Spreading the garment as well as she could with one hand, Jessie took a deep breath, then jammed the cloth against Mattie Lou's face, clamping her hand tightly over the woman's nose and mouth.

Mattie Lou jerked up and screamed, crying out in terror as she clawed at the thing shrouding her head. Jessie rolled free, slipped the papers quickly into their case, and slid it under the blanket. Scrambling to her knees, she scurried frantically for the flap of the tent. Too late, she saw the big shadow fall over the canvas. Turning on her heels, she dove for the cover of Mattie's trunks and drew herself into a ball.

"Christ, Mattie, what in hell's going on in here!" Cottonmouth Sully yelled as he stomped into the tent and came to a stop.

"Someone was—in here!" Mattie screeched. "They tried to kill me, Sully!"

Jessie heard Sully let out a breath. "There's no one here, Mattie. You had a nightmare or something. What's that thing?"

Mattie blinked at the garment clutched in her hands. "It's a dress," she said shortly. "What do you think it is?"

Sully laughed. "Well, there's your strangler, Mattie."

"I do not take my gowns to bed. Someone was in here, Sully!"

"Yeah, right. Go to sleep, okay?"

"Hell of a big help you are," Mattie grumbled.

Jessie didn't move. She waited, biting her lip until it hurt. Mattie began breathing in a slow, easy rhythm. Finally Jessie brought herself slowly erect, crawled to the entry and listened, then slid out into the darkness of the trees.

Sully's tent was dark. Still, something told her not to move. How did he get there so fast? He had to be up already, out there in the night . . .

Five minutes later she saw him. He was leaning against a tree to her left, not ten yards away, looking over the sleeping camp. Jessie backed through the trees and down the hill. When she reached the cover of the ravine she started shaking. She had perspired profusely, and her blouse clung wetly to her skin.

At the edge of the grove she stopped, peering cautiously through the trees. There was the dead fire and there was her blanket, and beyond the dim coals—Jessie suddenly went rigid. Harrow wasn't there, he was gone! A branch rubbed cloth not twenty feet away. A boot came down and crushed dry leaves. Jessie dropped quickly to the ground. An instant later, Harrow stepped into the open.

"Sue," he said evenly, "you want to tell me what the hell you're doing, wandering around in the dark? I'd be real interested to know."

"What does it look like?" Jessie said sharply. She came erect, jerking her denims quickly over bare legs and hips. "If I'd known you like to watch, I would've woken you!"

"Oh. I, uh—" Harrow cleared his throat and looked away. "Look, I saw you gone and I—"

"Yeah, thanks for your concern. All right with you if I finish up alone?"

Harrow let out a breath and retreated quickly through the brush. Jessie leaned against a tree, waiting for her legs to stop shaking.

She woke to the smell of bacon and fresh coffee, stretched and sat up, and saw Harrow watching her over the fire.

"Well," she said sleepily, "breakfast in bed. This is a pleasant surprise." She stood, scratched the back of her neck, and sat down across the fire, crossing her legs Indian-style. "You make good coffee. A lot better than mine."

"You haven't tasted it yet."

"Don't have to. I can tell by the smell." She found her cup and filled it with steaming coffee, then scraped bacon and bread onto her plate.

"Listen," he told her, "I'm sorry about last night."

"Forget it. You didn't know."

He looked up sheepishly, saw the sparkle in Jessie's eyes, and grinned.

"Hey, that's better," she said. "Didn't think you were going to show me a smile again. That's about the first time in two days, you know."

"Sue . . ." Harrow's face clouded.

97

"No, uh-uh. You don't have to say a thing."

"Yes, I do. I owe you an explanation."

"You don't owe me a thing," said Jessie. "It's me that owes you, remember? You've pulled me out of a bad scrape twice now, and I'm grateful." She caught his eyes, and looked at him without expression. "'Course, I got to say I'm surprised, you know? We were, uh, coming on sort of strong to each other a couple of days ago. Standing down by the river, if you recall."

"Sue, I *know* where it was," he snapped. "Damn it all, I—" He stopped and stood up. "We'll talk some later," he muttered. "I'm sorry. I got to get over to the flats. They've got some trouble with the wagons."

"Sure. Don't let me keep you." He turned to her again, and the look in his eyes told Jessie he wanted to stay.

"Go on," she said shortly, "I don't want to talk to you, John Harrow. I might say something I shouldn't!"

The moment he was gone, she clenched her fists and kicked the coffeepot savagely into the brush. She'd told herself from the start that Collier was right, getting close to John Harrow was business, part of what she was here to do. She knew, though, that that wasn't true. She might get friendly with a man, give him a saucy grin that said a lot, but if she crawled under his blanket there was only one reason: the honest pleasure a man and a woman could share. It was the way she'd always been; she couldn't change now and wouldn't try.

Doesn't look as if I've got to worry, one way or the other. Mr. John Fielding Harrow's not all that excited about Sue Deevers . . .

All morning she found reasons to keep an eye on Hager's camp. Barc's men were as thick as flies, and there was no way on earth to get close to Ki.

Jessie's nerves were rubbed raw. The information she'd risked her life to get was plain useless unless she could get it to the Rangers. According to Harrow, the outlaws would break camp in the morning. That meant stealing a horse and leaving *tonight;* any later and the whole thing would be lost.

At least, she reminded herself grimly, she knew a lot more than Collier had wanted to tell her. Nat hadn't figured on not making it back, and had seen no reason to share his outside contacts with Jessie and Ki. Captain Simms, though, had backed down when Jessie insisted.

From the moment Collier had learned about the outlaw gathering, it was clear that following his trail was too chancy to risk. The outlaws would be keeping their eyes open, letting no one close who didn't belong. Instead the Rangers would wait for Collier to get word out. There was a large force at Gonzales on the Guadalupe River, and another at a post on the Lavaca. Once the target was clear, they could burn up the wires across Texas, alerting every Ranger, sheriff, town constable, and federal outpost.

I've got to do it tonight, thought Jessie. *Only I can't leave without telling Ki. He'll think something's happened, that Mattie or Sully has found me out. And then he'll risk his life to help me, and they'll get him . . .*

Harrow came for her at noon. Jessie read his eyes at once and knew something was wrong.

"Come on," he said flatly. "We're going to see Mattie and Sully."

"What the hell for?" Jessie said bluntly. "The farther I am from those two, the better I like it."

"They want to see us. I don't know why, Sue."

He won't look right at me. Mattie or Sully saw me, and Harrow knows.

Harrow stalked across the flats ahead of her, keeping his eyes to the ground.

"Do you mind slowing down," Jessie asked irritably. "We running a race or something?"

"Sorry," Harrow muttered, but made no effort to slow his pace.

"Have you had anything to eat?"

"No, haven't had time."

"We'll put something together when we get back," she suggested. "I bought a couple of eggs off the wagon last night."

99

"Yeah, fine."

"John, just a minute." She grasped his arm and stopped him. "What is it? Tell me."

"Tell you what?"

"You're taking me to Mattie and Sully. You know I'm scared to death of that pair. I want to know *why* I'm going."

Harrow shook his head. "Sue, they're not going to pull any of that business again. It's over. I wouldn't let that happen. You think I would?"

"No," she said honestly, "I don't guess I do."

"Well, then. There's no reason to—"

"John!" Jessie saw the glint of metal on the hill, and half a second later heard the sharp crack of the rifle. She threw herself at him as the sound rolled over the flats. Harrow grunted and went down. The rifle roared again and again, raising plumes of dirt at Jessie's heels. She sprawled after Harrow and jerked the big revolver from his coat. Coming up in a crouch, she held the weapon out straight in both hands and squeezed off the entire cylinder toward the hill. Before the pistol clicked empty, another weapon joined Jessie's. She whirled around and saw Doc Holliday, his gaunt form shielding Harrow, calmly firing a Henry .44.

Holliday lowered the rifle, squinting at the side of the hill. "He's gone. Isn't coming back and he's got a good horse. You all right, John?"

Jessie knelt over Harrow, her braided hair brushing his chest.

"Yeah, I'm alive, I guess." He grinned painfully at Jessie. "Thanks. You've got a good eye."

"And you've got the luck of the devil," Jessie breathed. She put one hand under his shoulder and peeled off his jacket. The bullet had found the flesh at the edge of his chest beneath his arm, plowed a deep furrow, and kept going.

"You see who it was?" asked Harrow. "Or do I need to guess?"

"Know who it was," Doc said shortly. "That sorry bastard, Clay Allison. Figured he was studying on pulling out, and might want to kiss you goodbye. Sorry I was late." He glanced down at Jessie. "You sure do keep bad company, miss, if you don't mind me saying."

Jessie laughed. Her green eyes flashed at Harrow and he returned the look in kind. "Looks like I'm stuck with him awhile."

Chapter 14

Almost before Harrow was on his feet, the clearing was crowded with men brandishing rifles and pistols, all shouting at once. Cottonmouth Sully bulled his way through, took one look at Harrow's bloodied shirt, and turned angrily on the others.

"Go on, get the hell about your business!" he bellowed. "Right now, damn it! You hurt bad, John? Who was it, you know?"

"Clay Allison," Holliday drawled. "Miss Mattie's friend."

Sully reddened and shook his head. "Shit. Wish I'd never laid eyes on the bastard." He looked at Harrow, then glanced quickly at Jessie and turned his gaze back to Harrow. "Forget comin' over to Mattie's. Get that wound taken care of, and we'll talk later."

"Huh-uh." Harrow shook his head stubbornly. "She wants to talk, now's just fine with me. I got a patch of Sue's bandanna stuffed under my arm, and that'll hold."

"Suit yourself." Sully shrugged. "But don't blame me if Mattie makes you sicker. Goddamn woman's on a tear. The James boys have pulled out for sure, which you already know. She thinks they took Billy Bonney with 'em."

Harrow looked pained. "Christ, the Kid wasn't even here, Sul."

"Yeah, well, *you* tell her that." Sully moved off over the flats, Jessie and Harrow beside him, Doc Holliday bringing up the rear. Jessie noted that Sully hadn't asked Doc along, which apparently didn't bother the man at all.

Mattie Lou was stomping up and down in front of her tent, overdressed as usual, in a gown more fitting for the Governor's Ball than for a trek in the wilds. Jessie tried not

102

to stare. It was the first time she'd seen the woman on her feet, and the effect was almost frightening. With each cumbersome step, every part of her body rolled in a separate direction. Her tight yellow curls were in tangled disarray, her doughy features flushed fever-bright. At the sight of Sully and the others, her little eyes went wide.

"Someone fired shots," she blurted. "I heard shots, damn it! What's wrong, Sully, what is it!"

"Just take it easy. Clay Allison snapped off a couple at John. Nobody's hurt."

"Allison? Allison?" Mattie stared wildly at Harrow. "Christ, why'd he do that? I—I won't *have* it, Sully!"

"Mattie, he's gone. There's nothing we can do about it now."

Mattie didn't seem to hear. Her eyes swept suspiciously over Harrow, Holliday, and Jessie. "Someone got into my tent last night. Came in and tried to smother me to death in my bed! You got any idea who'd do a thing like that?" Her eyes bored straight into Jessie's. "How 'bout you, dearie? By God, I'll bet it was you, you little slut!"

"*Dearie,* you wouldn't catch me dead anywhere close to your bed," Jessie said flatly.

Mattie made a noise in her throat and came at her. Sully pushed her back and glared savagely at Harrow. "Damn it, tell your woman to keep her mouth shut!"

"Tell *that* one to watch what she says," Harrow said evenly.

Sully spoke close to Mattie's ear. Mattie glanced sullenly at Jessie, spittle flecking the corners of her mouth, then turned and waddled around her tent. Sully guided the others quickly away.

"She's upset about Frank and Jesse," he explained, "and I don't guess Allison's taking off helped."

"Someone really get in her tent?" asked Harrow.

"Beats hell out of me. Woke up hollerin', tangled up in her clothes. Don't take any offense, now. She's having me ask everyone. Your girl ain't been singled out."

Harrow stopped abruptly, his cool gray eyes locked on Sully's. "Is that what you brought us here for? 'Cause if it is—"

"Not you, John. Her. Your woman." Sully cursed under his breath. "Her, and anyone else Mattie don't particularly care for. Naw, she wants to talk to *you* about business. That can wait. No use bothering with it now." He looked narrowly at Jessie. "Stay clear of her, girl. That's just friendly advice."

"Mister, you can count on it," Jessie told him.

Sully left them and walked back. Doc Holliday took off his hat and wiped his brow. "John, that woman's the best reason I ever saw for becoming a monk. Damned if she isn't."

Harrow didn't smile. "Sully'll calm her down. He knows how to handle her."

"You mind if I say something?" Jessie spoke up. "It's none of my business, but I have to ask anyway."

"What?" said Harrow.

"About Mattie Lou. I'm not in the outlaw business, except kind of on the edge, but I hope I'm not a fool, either. Doesn't it bother you gents, a fat lady foaming at the mouth heading up this deal?"

Harrow went rigid; for a moment Jessie thought he might hit her. "You're right, Sue. It is *not* any of your goddamn business!" Holding his hand against his chest, he stalked away, leaving Jessie and Holliday.

"Well, I went and did it again," sighed Jessie. "Only I still think it's a real good question."

Doc Holliday grinned. "Yeah, it is that. Don't mind John, he's just got his dander up some. I'll tell you about Mattie Lou Lynn if you want to know."

"Yes, I *do* want to know," said Jessie.

"She owned a big saloon in San Francisco some years back. Put her income in trade and land and got rich, then piled money on top of money, banking fellows who needed a stake to pull a job—and charging a healthy interest for her troubles. Pretty soon she was planning the jobs herself, and taking a bigger piece. That's where she got hooked up with Sully."

"And she knows what she's doing, Doc?" Jessie asked skeptically.

"Oh, yes." Doc took out a cheroot and rolled it between his fingers. "She's good at it. Just doesn't act like it, is all. Mattie Lou Lynn's a...criminal genius, you might say." A small grin touched the corner of his mouth. "Don't mean she isn't crazy, though, 'cause she is."

Jessie left Doc and walked back alone. She still wasn't convinced about Mattie. If she was a "criminal genius," as Holliday said, would the cartel trust her, knowing she could step over the line into madness at any moment? But if Mattie wasn't in charge, who was? Not Sully—he was a number-two man and nothing more. And that left Harrow, whether Jessie liked it or not.

If that's true, he and Mattie and Sully are playing a game in front of me and everyone else. And a damn good one, too!

By late afternoon, everyone was packing his gear for the five-mile ride from the practice area back to the encampment. It was no secret now that they'd be leaving for the target in the morning. Every man Jessie saw seemed to move a little faster. They were ready, tired of waiting for the big day to come.

Jessie knew exactly how she was going to get away. She'd wandered about all she could, keeping her eyes open. There was no other way, no matter how many times she chewed it around. The communal corral was always under guard. The only way to get a horse was to take one from the outriders' camp. They constantly prowled the land for miles around, keeping the area free of intruders. They kept their small corral a mile out, along with a place to get coffee after their shift. Jessie figured they wouldn't be looking for trouble. It was a risk, but there was no other way. Jessie prayed that Ki would guess what she'd done—that she'd found what they were after.

Now all I've got to do is hope Harrow sleeps soundly. Lord, I think the man keeps one eye open all night!

"Sue—I was hopin' I could see you 'fore we all rode back!"

* * *

Jessie started and looked up from her packing. "Cindy, I've been trying to see *you*, but you never seem to be around."

"Oh, I've been *around*, all right," she said wearily, knotting her fingers in the cloth of her shirt. "But they're givin' me a real hard time. I can't even breathe without Red or Barc asking why."

Jessie stood, looked thoughtfully at the girl, and saw the fear in her eyes. "It's bad, isn't it? Did something happen, something that—"

"Oh, yeah, somethin' *happened*, all right," Cindy said warily. "Only thing is, I ain't real sure whether Red and Barc know it, or whether they're just guessing."

Jessie looked blank, and Cindy went on quickly. "Remember I told you I found someone real special—not like the others at all?"

"Uh-huh. Only you never got around to saying who."

Cindy turned pale. "God A'mighty, Sue, I'm almost 'fraid to say it out loud. I think maybe they're going to kill me or something. No—I'm damn certain they are!"

"Cindy—" Jessie gripped the girl's shoulders to stop her shaking. "Just tell me what happened, all right?"

"I, uh—my man and me went up the river and we— you know. I'm sure Red don't know, Sue, but if he just *thinks* he does, it's the same. Barc's madder'n hell about something—I never seen him like this before. God, if I'm right, he'll shoot me and Chang both!"

Jessie's mouth fell open. *"Who!"*

"See? I knew you wouldn't believe it," Cindy moaned. "He's not like he seems at all, honest. Get him off alone and he's a different person, a— Sue, you look worse than me!"

"No, I'm fine," Jessie said shakily. "It's just been one hell of a day, is all."

Harrow emptied his coffee in the last embers of the fire, scratched his chest, and yawned. "I guess it's a fool thing to say, but I feel better getting back near the river. That doesn't make sense, does it? One campsite's the same as the next."

"Yeah, I guess," said Jessie.

Harrow was silent for a long moment. Jessie felt his eyes on her, but didn't look up. The campground was quiet. The outlaws had celebrated the start of the big raid, drinking up everything in camp as quickly as they could. A few hearty souls still staggered about, but most of the men had taken to their blankets or passed out under a tree.

"I think maybe you and me better talk," Harrow said finally. "I've got a couple of things I want to get straight."

"Good," Jessie said absently. "How about first thing in the morning?"

"No. In the morning won't do, and you know it."

Jessie looked up. His features were hazy, indistinct in the darkness, but there was no mistaking the determination in his voice. "All right. Talk, then."

"You're still put out with me, aren't you?"

"No, I— Yeah, I guess maybe I am. But don't let it bother you, friend. It's not real important anymore, is it?"

"I think it is," Harrow said sharply. "Sue—" Suddenly he moved from his side of the fire and grabbed her roughly in his arms. Jessie gasped, caught her breath, and pulled angrily out of his grip.

"Why the sudden interest?" she snapped. "You get a 'manly urge' or something, Mr. Harrow?"

His features went rigid, then relaxed. "All right. I had that coming. Now. Will you sit still and listen a minute?"

"I'm listening."

He reached out and gripped her shoulders, and this time she didn't protest. "You said it yourself, so I don't have to tell you. We had us a minute or so together by the river, and then—nothing after that."

"Yes. I kind of noticed."

"Just shut up," he said fiercely, "all right?" He brought her to him, crushing his mouth against her lips until Jessie gasped for air.

"That didn't feel to me like talking!" she gasped when he released her.

"It's the kind of talking we should've been doing all along, Sue. I know that and so do you."

"I haven't exactly been running from you," Jessie said

107

coolly. "You're the one that stopped being interested, John. That's your privilege. You sure don't owe me any favors, and I don't much like you changing your mind in midstream!"

Harrow looked pained. "Sue, look—"

"No. *You* look, mister. I felt something for you. And I guess maybe I still do. Only it's a little late now."

"You are not going to listen to me, are you?"

"Listen to what? That we're breaking camp in the morning, and all of a sudden you feel like a little lovin'? No thanks, mister. When I—"

Harrow cut off her words with his mouth, covering her face with kisses. His hands circled her waist and drew her to him, forcing her to the ground with his weight. "You little fool," he said sharply, "I've been staying away from you because I *do* care, Sue. I feel something I haven't felt before, and I'm damned if I know what to do with it. I want you so much, I've done everything I could to push you out of my life. Does that make any sense at all?"

"Yes, I—guess maybe it does," Jessie said weakly.

★

Chapter 15

"Just tell me you don't want me," Harrow whispered. "Tell me that and I'll leave you alone."

"If I told you that, I'd be lying," said Jessie, "but to-night's just not the— Oh, Lord, John, what are you *doing!*"

Harrow came to his knees, gripped Jessie firmly, and lifted her off the ground. The stars whirled dizzily overhead as he carried her away from the camp and into the trees. Jessie clung to him, feeling the rapid beating of his heart against her cheek. When he found the spot he wanted, he laid her down gently and knelt beside her. The grove of ancient oaks formed a nearly solid wall around them. The moon cast a muted, silvery light through the tangled branches above.

"I found this place the other day," he told her. "I wanted to bring you here then."

"It's real nice," she said. "Doesn't even feel like we're anywhere near all—all of them."

Harrow's face came closer. Jessie saw a vein pulse rapidly in his throat, felt the touch of his breath against her cheek. He cupped her chin in his hand and kissed her lightly, a slow and gentle kiss that barely brushed her flesh. Jessie closed her eyes as he found the corner of her mouth. Her lips parted slightly and the tip of her tongue flicked out to find him. He took the soft offering and drew it between his lips. Jessie trembled and stirred against him, sliding her hands along the corded sinews of his arms and the broad slope of his shoulders. His muscles tensed, growing as hard as iron. He drew her closer and ground his mouth against hers, forcing her lips fully open. Jessie opened her mouth eagerly to let him in, drinking in the man-taste of his kiss.

109

Harrow moaned deeply within his chest, letting his mouth trail quickly down the slim column of her throat to the swell of her breasts. Stroking her neck softly with one hand, he reached up with the other to undo the tiny buttons of her blouse.

Jessie's breath quickened at his touch. She brushed her hands past the fabric of his shirt to his head, twisting her fingers tightly through his hair. She felt his hands tremble as he loosened the blouse to her waist, then slipped his hands beneath the cloth to bring the garment off her shoulders.

"Wait . . . wait," she whispered, bringing up her hands to press him gently away.

Harrow stopped. "What is it, Sue? Don't you—"

"Just *wait,*" she insisted, "and you'll see. All right? Trust me about five minutes, Mr. Harrow."

"Four, maybe."

Jessie laughed and rolled out of his grasp, then sprang to her feet and faced him. "See, I've been thinking about you, too. Kind of waiting for a moment like this."

"You have, have you?"

"Oh, yes. I surely have, John Harrow." Matching his bold look with her own, she stepped up to him, one loose sleeve of her blouse draping provacatively over her shoulder. It slid to the swell of her breast and she made no effort to retrieve it. Looking straight at him, she reached up to grasp the first button of his shirt. Harrow's eyes went wide with surprise as he realized what she was doing.

"Don't mind, do you? If you do, I'll sure stop."

"No, uh—don't do that," he said dryly.

Jessie laughed at his expression and loosed one button and then another. A light matting of hair covered his chest, and she teased it with her fingers. "I mean it, now. I'll quit if you want, John."

"You know damn well what my answer is to that."

"Thought you might think I was kind of—forward, you know? Some fellows might figure it's unladylike for a girl to strip down a man. *I* think turnabout's fair play."

Harrow took a breath and held it as she loosened the last

110

button and drew the tail of his shirt out of his trousers. Running her hand up the full length of his chest, she eased the shirt off his shoulders and let it slide free. The sight of him naked to the waist stirred feelings deep within her. He was lean and hard-bodied, his solid flesh molded in slabs of muscle over his shoulders and down his chest to the flat plane of his belly.

"You are a fine-looking man," she said softly. "I sure do like what I see. So far, that is. There's still some to go."

"I, uh—don't intend to disappoint you."

"Oh, my." Jessie bit her lip and gave him a saucy wink. "Hope you can live up to all this bragging."

Standing nearly against him, she playfully freed the buckle of his belt. Then, going to her knees, she loosed the buttons of his trousers, slipping each one aside and taking her time, pausing a long moment between one and the next. She could feel his member swelling, hardening like steel beneath the restraining cloth. Still, she carefully avoided his erection, knowing he sensed her fingers so near that she could reach out and grasp him if she liked.

"Lady, are you trying to kill me or what?" rasped Harrow. "Damn, Sue..."

"Why, I'm not even touching you," Jessie told him. "How could a man die of that?"

"Real easy. Just stick around and watch."

"Another couple of buttons," she whispered. "That one, and then—there. Oh, Lord—you've been keeping something from me, John!" Jessie felt the heat rise to her face as his erection sprang free. The spear of his manhood was now only inches from her face. Her pulse beat rapidly in her throat. With trembling hands she slid his trousers down over his hips. He rested his hands on her shoulders as she bent to take off his boots and help him kick his trousers away. She looked at him then, towering naked above her in the dim light of the grove. The sight left her breathless, too weak to move. His power seemed to glow on the surface of his flesh, a dim aura that drained her of strength. Moving her hands across the earth, she grasped his legs and pulled herself up to his thighs. The heavy scent of his maleness assailed her senses, quickened her excitement. Sliding her hands over the hard mounds of his buttocks, she circled his waist and gently kissed the dark matting below his belly. Harrow shuddered at her touch and cupped the back of her neck between his hands. Jessie's kisses slid like velvet over his skin, burning where they touched. When her lips found the base of his shaft, Harrow gave a quick sigh of pleasure. Jessie's own excitement quickened, smoldered in her thighs, and raced to the points of her breasts. Her lips moved like a whisper along his length; the tip of her tongue snaked out to tease him, stroke him gently, then flick shyly away. Finally she brought her hands from his waist to hold him gently on the tips of her fingers. Wetting her tongue, she lightly kissed the swollen head of his member, then let his length slide swiftly past her lips.

Harrow went rigid; his whole body shuddered, and Jessie felt every cord and tendon tighten with pleasure. She kneaded him with her tongue, relishing each stroke that brought the satin touch of his flesh against her own. Harrow caressed her hair with his hands, caught the rhythm of her desire, and pressed himself gently into the furnace of her mouth. Jessie sensed the quickening of his thrusts, the mounting hunger in his loins. She stroked his back, molding her body against his legs, straining to take him ever deeper. Harrow groaned, and she slid her hands up his thighs to rake sharp nails across his buttocks. He trembled and sucked in air; a ragged moan came from deep within his chest.

Jessie held him tight as he filled her with his warmth. She clung to him, her lips encircling his flesh. Liquid fire seemed to surge through her body, setting every nerve screaming with desire. Suddenly the taste of his liquid essence triggered her own release, lifting her up on a crest of pain and pleasure. She continued to hold him in her mouth as one jolting spasm followed another.

Harrow pulled away and lifted her in his arms and carried her slender form beneath the trees. Jessie looked up and gave him a lazy smile. She saw her own joy reflected in his eyes, the look that told her he knew the pleasure she'd brought him had met her needs as well.

"Sue," he said gently, "I have never wanted a woman

more, and none has ever given me such pleasure. Do you believe that?"

"It's a nice thing to say," she told him, lightly touching her finger to his cheek. "And yes—I think I do believe you, John."

"You'd better," he said firmly. "It's not a thing I'd say lightly."

"Well, I didn't exactly suffer much myself. I guess maybe you noticed."

Harrow tried to look puzzled. "Notice what? Did I miss something?"

"Bastard!" Jessie bit her lip and pounded his chest until he covered her small fists with his own.

"Next time I'll pay more attention," he said soberly. "I'm a man who likes to know what's going on around him."

"Huh!" Jessie pouted. "And who said there's going to *be* a next time, Mr. Harrow?"

"*I* did," he said, giving her his best ferocious frown. "Damn, lady, you know how embarrassing it is—a naked man running around with a fully clothed woman?"

"You didn't act all that humiliated a minute ago."

"That's only because you, uh—distracted me for a while."

"That's what I did, huh? Distracted you?"

"Some. Not much, of course."

"Hah!" Jessie scoffed, planting a hard kiss on his mouth. "Sure looked different from where I was. Near as I could tell, you were— *John*, oh, Lord, what are you trying to do!"

Harrow dropped to his knees, set her roughly on her bottom, and stripped her blouse the rest of the way off. Tossing it away, he attacked the buttons of her denims, nearly popping them as he pulled the fly apart. Jessie was glad she'd left her ivory-handled derringer tucked in the folds of her bedroll; it would have been a difficult thing to explain at a moment like this . . .

Flipping her over on her stomach, he planted one foot on her buttocks and pulled off first one of her boots, then the other. Jessie couldn't believe he was treating her this way, but resistance was the furthest thing from her mind. In fact, as far as she was concerned, he couldn't get her

113

clothes off her fast enough. Ripples of heat surged through her as he grabbed the cuffs of her jeans and pulled upward, dumping her on the ground.

She lay limp, gasping, as he stood above her, shaking his head in wonder at the lovely sight before him. "By God," he said breathlessly, "if I didn't unwrap me a pretty package."

Harrow came down beside her, letting his eyes wander boldly over her body. It was a look so intense that Jessie could almost feel it caressing her flesh. He stared at her incredibly long legs, his gaze moving past the lush curve of her hips and resting longingly on the soft, feathery patch between her thighs. She could feel him there, as if his member were already deep within her. He touched her then, letting his fingers stroke the velvety mounds of her breasts.

"Yes, oh, *yes!*" Jessie moaned. She arched her back off the ground, twisting in a sensuous curve beneath his touch. The motion hollowed her belly and thrust her breasts up to meet him. She reached out to grasp his cheeks within her hands, drawing him closer to her.

"Will you kiss me?" she whispered. "Kiss my breasts, please!"

He held her waist and brought his lips softly against the firm swell of her flesh. Jessie opened her mouth and sighed. With the tip of his tongue he traced the dusky shadow circling her breast. The pattern of his touch grew ever smaller until he moistened the dimpled flesh and gently caressed her nipple.

"Oh, my . . ." Jessie's breath came faster. Her breasts rose under his touch, thrusting eagerly against his lips. He supped on the ivory spheres between his hands, drawing each pointy nipple into his mouth. Jessie trembled, twisting her body beneath him. With each new touch she felt the fires churning within her. She wrapped her arms about his neck, bringing the slender length of her body firmly against him. She could feel his hardness now, the press of his erection between her thighs. The silver glow of the moon seemed to turn her body to liquid, melting her flesh into his. She pressed his head to her breasts, urging him to draw the pliant nipples into his mouth. Now even the slightest touch of his tongue made her gasp. She thrashed beneath

114

him, grinding her silken mound against his member. He answered her hunger at once, parting her legs with his own to rest the underside of his shaft gently against her.

Jessie cried out at his touch. She caressed him with the moist folds of her pleasure, arching her back to bring her closer, taunting him with the promise of greater delights. Harrow matched her game, pausing to tease her first at one secret place and then another. She felt his body begin to tremble, harden with the tension that sang between them. She longed to feel him inside her, to scissor her legs about him and send him plunging into her warmth. Each stroke of his member was an agony of delight, an exquisite taste of joys to come. The heat of their passion formed a light film of moisture between them. The slick feel of his flesh quickened Jessie's hunger and she cried out aloud.

"Now, John, now! Get inside me, love...deep, deep inside me!"

Harrow flinched at her words, grinding his erection roughly against her. Jessie threw back her head and gasped for breath. Harrow gripped her shoulders and drew away for an instant. Jessie clawed the flesh of his back, knowing what was coming. His fingers found the hot silken nest, parted the feathery curls, and let his fingers glide inside.

Jessie quivered and held him tight. "I—can't take that, John. I'm—I'm gonna tighten up and snap in two, and then you'll be sorry!"

"Guess I would be," he grinned. "Never saw a lady do that..."

"Well, just keep your eyes open, friend. I'm about to have a— Oh, Lord! No, please!" She thrashed wildly against him, but Harrow pushed her back with a firm but gentle touch between her breasts. Jessie opened her mouth, lips stretched tight against her teeth. Gently Harrow caressed the sweet flesh between her thighs, carefully avoiding the point where Jessie wanted him most. She clenched her fists at her sides, her breath coming in rapid bursts. His fingers teased her, circled the firm center of her delight, brushed it lightly, but never near enough. Jessie felt the sting of sweat on her brow. Harrow taunted the honeyed flower, his fingers moving closer and closer to the crown. Once more,

Jessie felt the fires of release burning within her. Her nails clawed at the earth. She squeezed her eyes shut; hot sparks danced across her vision. Her body arched off the ground on the columns of her legs, thrusting the heart of her pleasure up to meet him. She begged him to finish, pleaded for release.

"There—it's happening . . . now . . . now . . . now!"

His fingers closed gently on the hard, swollen pearl, teasing it as his mouth had teased her nipples. Jessie's whole body trembled—she writhed her mound against him, feeling the pleasure surging up inside her.

Suddenly John stopped, drawing his fingers away. Jessie opened her eyes and stared. "No, please. I'm there . . . I'm almost there!"

Harrow grinned, grasped her hips roughly in his hands, and thrust his member inside her without warning . . .

Jessie screamed and bit her lip, bringing a coppery taste of blood. The power of her orgasm wrenched every fiber of her being, tore her apart and left her shattered. She shook uncontrollably, only dimly aware that he'd emptied himself inside her once more. One wave of pleasure after another lifted her up and tossed her aside, each spasm stronger than the last. She knew she couldn't stop them, and for a quick, terrifying moment she was certain the frenzied explosions would seize her heart, kill her in one last thunderous avalanche of joy . . .

Jessie was only dimly aware that he had dressed, then slipped her into her clothes and lifted her up in his arms. A deep and syrupy warmth enveloped her body, as if a thousand tiny fires were banked inside her. She leaned against his chest, dozing lazily to the rhythm of his walk. When he lowered her to the blanket at their camp, she opened her eyes and blinked, startled to find him there.

"Take a little rest, did you?" he whispered. "Thought I'd lost you for a minute."

"I thought so too," she sighed. "That was sure fine loving, Mr. Harrow. Fine loving indeed."

"Sue—" He dropped down beside her, nestling her head in the hollow of his shoulder. "I'm going to ask you some-

116

thing and I want you to keep still and listen till I finish. Will you do that?"

"Yes. All right, John."

He took a deep breath and brought her cheek closer against him. "When this business is over, I want you to come with me. Back East somewhere, maybe. It doesn't matter where—"

"John!" Jessie raised her head and stared. "Wh-what are you trying to say?"

"Let me finish," he said firmly. "All I'm saying is I think we make a good pair. We could try it out, see what happens. No strings attached. I don't think either of us is cut out for that." He leaned over and kissed her. "But it might be nice, you know? We could have some good times, and I'll promise you one thing, lady. I'd be good to you. You'd never have to worry about that."

Jessie tried to hold back the tears, but they came rushing out in a flood. Harrow crushed her to him, cradling her in his arms.

"Hey now, there's no call for that. Damn, I never can tell with women—are you happy or sad?"

"Hell, I don't know. Some of both, maybe." She touched his cheek and kissed him. "I—can't talk about this now, all right? I just can't. Try to understand that, will you?"

"'Course I understand," he said gently. "You don't have to say a thing. Get some sleep now, all right?" He smiled and ran his fingers over her breasts. "We had a busy night, and we've got one hell of a busy day ahead."

"Yeah," she said dryly, staring past him in the dark, "we do for a fact..."

She looked up at the stars, feeling the comforting warmth of his body close beside her. His chest rose and fell in a slow and easy rhythm, and she knew he was sinking into a deep sleep.

And when you're asleep, John, I'll get up and leave you and you'll never see me again. Because I'm not Sue Deevers and I didn't come here to make love to John Harrow. I came here to stop you, to put you behind bars or get you shot down in the street...

117

She almost cried out aloud in sorrow and anger. She couldn't betray him. Not now, not after tonight. He'd saved her life, taken her in with no questions asked. Somehow she had to warn him, keep him from riding with the others.

And what if you're right? she asked herself dully. *What if he is the cartel's agent?* She knew the answer all too well. She'd betray a lot more than John Harrow. She'd betray Ki, herself, everything her father had fought and died for.

She took a deep breath, forcing the pain and sorrow from her mind. There was no answer, no way to make it right.

She knew he was safely asleep. Still, she sat up slowly, listening to his breathing for a long moment. Slipping the blanket quietly aside, she eased the derringer from the spot where she'd hidden it, tucked it in the waistband of her jeans, and got to her knees. Her boots were by her side. She'd carry them until she was well into the woods, past the main encampment, close to the spot where the outriders kept their horses. She prayed that the off-duty guards would be sleeping as soundly as Harrow. If they weren't, she—

A terrible scream ripped through the night, and then another and another. Harrow jerked up straight beside her. "Good God," he blurted, "what the hell's that!" Almost at once, lanterns bobbed through the trees, moving down the path close to the river.

Jessie nodded dumbly, too frightened to move. Harrow came to his feet and walked through the trees, collaring the first man he saw. "What is it?" he asked sharply. "What's going on down there?"

The man blinked and took a breath. "They say some goddamn chink went crazy," he said excitedly. "Killed Barc Hager and his woman, and cut up another feller bad. Better get down there, mister, or we're going to miss the hanging!"

★

Chapter 16

Ki cursed under his breath and started yanking pots and pans from the horse's pack. The animal wore a makeshift canvas blanket fitted with loops, pockets, and leather straps. Twice a day Ki fixed meals at the camp, loaded pots of beans, hot coffee, and bread in the proper loops, and walked the horse to the spot where Barc's men practiced for the raid.

Ki walked, and the food rode. There were plenty of extra mounts, but none for Chinese cooks. The portable kitchen was Red's way of keeping him hopping, eighteen hours a day.

He was wringing wet, but he didn't dare drop under a tree and relax. One of Barc's men was close by, and he'd delight in telling Red that the cook was sleeping on the job.

Lugging his pans to the creek, he searched the narrow valley for Jessie. He'd seen her three times that morning, twice the day before. She was doing all she could to get to him, that was as clear as rainwater. Did she know something? Was she in some kind of danger?

Late in the afternoon, Ki heard shots up the valley— rifles exchanging fire and then the rapid cracks of a pistol. Moments later, two of Barc's men rode in and he heard what had happened. Allison had tried to kill John Harrow. Harrow's woman and Doc Holliday had driven him off, and the man was gone for good.

Ki turned away, every muscle in his body tight with frustration and anger. Christ, Jessie trading shots with one of the worst sons of bitches in the West, and what was *he* doing? Scraping dried beans off a pot! The thought brought

119

him shame and a fresh surge of fury. He had sworn on his honor as a samurai to protect her, given Jessie's father his solemn oath. And now he was useless, no good to her at all. They could kill her, do whatever they liked, and he'd be too late to stop them...

Cindy found him in the trees, where he was gathering wood for the fire. Ki stood as he saw her coming, caught the fear in her eyes, and saw the ugly bruise across her cheek. He dropped the wood and took her in his arms, pulling her quickly out of sight.

"Cindy—what happened? Who was it? Red?"

Cindy shook her head, scalding his chest with tears. Ki held her away and wiped her eyes with his shirt. "It wasn't Red, it was Barc," she moaned. "But Red started it all, damn him! Oh, Lord, Chang— you got to get me outa here. Please! We'll—we'll steal a horse or something, we—He's going to kill me, I *know* it!"

"Cindy—"

"He's been—asking funny questions, you know?"

"What kind of questions?"

"Like—who've I been fooling around with. *That* kind of question."

Ki looked at her. "He can't know anything about that, Cindy."

"Oh? You don't think so?" Her eyes bored into his. "What if Red knows, or somebody else?"

Ki read the desperation in her eyes. It didn't much matter whether she was imagining things or not. She was scared half out of her wits. "All right," he told her, "we'll do something. Tomorrow, maybe. I can—"

"No!" Cindy's eyes went wide. "We'll all be *leaving* tomorrow. I heard Barc say so! That means everyone'll get drunker'n hell tonight. And when Barc starts drinking—"

"Wait." Ki grabbed her shoulders and stared. "You're sure of that, Cindy? Tomorrow? Whatever they're going to do is *tomorrow?*"

"'Course I'm sure. Don't you see now? We can't wait, Chang. God, I'm so scared I'm 'bout to pee in my pants!"

Jessie knows! That's why she's trying to get to me! "Yes,

you're right," he said aloud. "We can't wait until tomorrow."

He didn't see her again until evening. Red stormed in, whipping his horse to a lather, and roared at Ki to get packed and move everything back to the encampment by the river. Ki obeyed, working so fast that even Red couldn't complain. A plan had been forming in his mind since he'd left Cindy in the woods. If she was right, everyone in camp who could beg or borrow a bottle would be roaring drunk after supper. He'd get her away in the confusion, find Jessie, and take them all out before anyone was the wiser. It made good sense, and he was determined to make Jessie see it. If she had information, fine. If not, it was sure as hell too late now. He wasn't about to let her ride out with Harrow and the others and get herself shot. And he never even considered leaving Cindy McGuire behind; he knew without asking that Jessie would feel the same.

It's over. By God, it's almost over, and not a minute too soon...

Ki cleared the ruins of supper in record time, dismantled the cookshack, and packed away his supplies. He left out the things he'd need for breakfast, though he didn't plan to be there for that event. Red ambled over and inspected Ki's work, his little pig eyes narrowed in a frown.

"You'll be ridin' ass-end tomorrow," he said harshly, "with the baggage and the whores. You get us fed fast, put away your shit, and sit still till I come and tell you different. You got all that?"

"Oh, yes." Ki bowed and gave Red a gracious smile. "Chang understand."

"Good. Make damn sure you do." Red grinned, doubled up his fist, and buried it in Ki's belly. Ki folded and went down hard. The blow came too fast for him to move, and he took its full force without warning.

Red laughed deep in his throat. "Chinks don't remember real good 'less you give 'em a little help. Ain't that right, Chang?"

Ki came shakily to his knees and retched in the dirt.

121

"I said, ain't that *right*, boy?"

"I—yes, I—"

Red kicked him in the side and sent him sprawling. Ki gasped and rolled away, tucking his head in against the next blow. Red didn't move. Ki saw him through a thick veil of pain that threatened to pull him under.

"Shit, I ain't goin' to kick you again," Red growled. "Not 'less you need it." He walked up and rolled Ki over with his boot. "Look at me, boy. Get your hands off your face and look right at me."

Ki backed off and stared straight in the man's eyes. Red had left him too numb to move, but there were reserves of strength left, smoldering deep within him. A samurai's mind controlled his body, and Ki could make his body work, do what it had to do...

Red squatted down so close to him that Ki could smell the whiskey on his breath. "Now listen to me real good," he said softly. "You got somethin' you might like to tell me? Somethin' maybe ol' Red ought to know?"

Every muscle in Ki's body went rigid. A sly, knowing grin touched the corners of Red's mouth.

"You done something you maybe hadn't ought to've done? Is that true, Chink?" Ki shook his head dumbly and brought fright and confusion to his eyes. "If you have, now, you tell Red and I won't hurt you no more. It'll be our secret, all right?"

"I—Chang does not understand..."

"Naw, of course Chang don't. You bastards don't understand nothing you don't want to, do you?",Red's features went hard. His heavy boot lashed out savagely again and again. Ki covered himself as well as he could, fighting to keep the dark from closing in...

He dragged himself through the brush, squeezing his eyes open and shut to drive the nausea away. *Hand down, lift the knee forward, bring up the other hand*...Every move was an agonizing effort. He stopped, tried to suck in air. Fire lanced through his lungs and he nearly cried out.

After a moment he found the trees and let himself rest. He could hear the voices from Barc's camp, see the bright glow of the fire. A bottle shattered against a rock and the men laughed.

Ki closed his eyes and took deep, regular breaths. Sweat beaded in droplets on his brow. A soothing warmth began to flood through his body, spreading to every bruised muscle and tendon. Slowly the pain began to subside. He willed it further away, pushed it back until it was a low, throbbing ache. The hurt was still there, but now it belonged to another person, a part of him he put aside for the moment. That person did not have the strength to find Jessie, to get Cindy away and escape from the encampment.

Pulling himself up against the tree, he flexed his arms and legs, rubbed them until they started working again. Jessie wouldn't be easy, but she was no problem at all compared to Cindy. Red watched her like a hawk, and now Barc was a problem as well. At the moment he would have given a great deal for a weapon—the deadly, trident-shaped *sai* or his slender *tanto* blade. But everything he owned was in a bundle back in Galveston. He'd known from the beginning that going armed into the outlaw camp was too great a risk. If they found such weapons on a Chinese cook...

Ki came suddenly alert. The shadow moved swiftly toward him through the trees. He went to a crouch, bringing his hands up high.

"Chang? Oh, Lord, are you in there somewhere?"

"Cindy?" Ki rose to his full height as the girl flung herself into his arms. "Cindy, I was just coming to find you. How did—"

"Are you all right?" she said anxiously. "Are you hurt real bad?"

"I'm hurt some, yes, but— Oh, Christ, Cindy!" Ki's flesh crawled as the truth suddenly struck him. He gripped her shoulders and held her away. "How did you know I was hurt?" he demanded. "Who told you?"

"One of the men—he said Red had hurt you real bad, that someone better—Chang, what are you looking at me like that for?"

"Don't ask questions," he said shortly. "Just take my hand and don't talk. Come *on,* damn it!" He ran through the trees for the river, knowing they'd never make it, that

123

Red had set it all up, given him the beating, then—

"Hold it, chink! Don't move a goddamn inch!"

Ki froze. Cindy choked off a cry and wrapped her arms tightly about him. Two shadows stepped out of the brush. Red poked his rifle at Ki's chest and grinned. "Shit, now ain't this a sight? There's your little whore, Barc, and her slant-eye lover. What'd I tell you now?"

Barc's features twisted in a mask. An angry cry exploded in his throat and he rushed past Red and tore the girl from Ki's grasp. Cindy screamed and Barc cut off her cries with a savage blow. Ki moved, but Red's Winchester was faster.

"Don't try it," he warned. "You'll make it too damn easy."

Ki backed off. Barc slung Cindy roughly over his shoulder, her legs flailing wildly in the air. Ki watched, gauging his chances of getting the weapon, and knew Red was praying for him to try.

A hush fell over Barc's crew as he stepped into the circle of the fire and dumped Cindy on the ground like a sack. Cindy moaned, clawed at the dirt, and tried to pull herself away. Barc kicked her in the belly; his eyes flashed and spittle fell from his mouth. He swayed once, stumbled, and nearly fell over his feet. Ki could see now that whiskey had helped to fuel his anger.

"Screw a goddamn chink, will you!" he raged. "Who else have you fucked, huh? Who, damn you!" His boots slammed viciously into her ribs. He kicked her again and again until his face glistened with sweat. Cindy cried out in pain, and Barc kicked her harder. Spreading his legs wide, he wrenched the nearly limp form off the ground and started ripping her dress from her body. Cindy tried to flee, but Barc cuffed her across the cheek. In a moment she was sprawled on her belly in the dirt, the firelight turning her naked flesh red. Hager gathered up torn shreds of her dress, stuffed a wad roughly in her mouth, then jerked her hands behind her and bound them tight.

Ki watched in horror on his knees, Red's rifle muzzle hard against his skull. Barc stumbled away from the fire, found Red's whip in the crook of a tree, and stalked back to the circle. His eyes swept the silent circle of his men,

124

the skin around his mouth stretched white.

"You *all* had her, didn't you?" he bawled drunkenly. "Every damn one of you, right? You lousy bunch of bastards!"

"Boss," one of the men said quietly, "there isn't a man here who'd—"

Barc cut him off with a glare. He pointed the coiled whip at Ki. "You watch now, Chink. You watch real close. The slut comes first, then I got somethin' special for you."

Barc raised the whip and brought it down hard on Cindy's back. An angry red welt appeared on her flesh. The leather lashed out again and again, striping her back with blood. Cindy's body jerked. She couldn't speak, but her eyes showed her terror through a veil of red hair. Barc wiped sweat off his brow and rolled the girl over on her back. Several men in the circle muttered softly at the sight. Barc stepped back, raised the whip over his head, and brought it down hard.

Ki moved!

In a single motion he spun on the balls of his feet, slammed the rifle from Red's hand, and jerked his elbow back like a hammer. Red grunted and stumbled back, his mouth spouting blood. An outlaw clawed for his pistol and Ki struck out in a blur, catching the man's cheek with the edge of his palm. He sensed rather than saw a man coming up behind him, whirled about in a quick half circle, and came off the ground. His foot lashed out and caught the man squarely in the gut. The man gasped and clutched his belly. Ki kicked him solidly in the throat and heard bone snap.

Barc's whip caught him by surprise—the rawhide snaked about his chest and jerked him to the ground. Ki rolled and came to his feet as leather stung his cheek, drawing blood. Barc laughed, snapped the whip off the ground, and lashed out again. Ki sprang deftly aside, caught the whiplash in his fist, and yanked hard. Barc stared as the weapon came out of his grasp. Ki threw it at Barc's face and came at him in a crouch. Barc swung a haymaker and missed. Ki moved low and fast, lashing out with short, punishing blows that rocked Barc on his heels. He swung wildly at Ki, but Ki moved his head aside and let the blows pass. Ki's right fist darted out, drove solidly into the man's solar plexus. Barc

125

staggered. His mouth went slack and the color drained from his face. Ki's left came up in a movement too fast for the eye to follow. His fingers were slightly bent, the joints a tight wedge of bone and cartilage. The blow darted in and out, Ki's rigid fingertips striking the point directly between Barc's windpipe and his chin. Barc's eyes bugged out, then went dim as the life left his body. Ki turned, bent in a fighting crouch, before the body slumped to the ground. Red hit him hard, launching the full weight of his body off the dirt and slamming Ki across the clearing. Ki twisted in midair, using the other's power to fling himself free. Red sprawled in the dust and sprang to his feet. The men stepped up quickly, leveling their weapons at Ki's head.

"No," Red growled harshly, waving them angrily away. "I want this bastard for myself!"

The cords in his massive neck tightened. He reached behind him and whipped a big bowie knife from his belt. Ki stepped back, giving the weapon the respect it deserved. The blade was a good twelve inches long, a heavy, well-honed weapon made for killing.

Ki watched Red closely, studying his stance and motions. In spite of the man's size, he moved with the fluid power of a cat; the way he held the knife told Ki he'd used it before.

Red prowled the clearing, firelight glinting off the blade and his piglike eyes. The long knife wavered like a snake, stabbing at the air to draw Ki's attention.

Ki didn't look at the blade. He kept his eyes on Red's arms, the muscles in his shoulders. The tendons in his wrist went tight and Ki moved, dancing deftly aside as the blade lashed out. Red grinned, feinted at Ki's belly, bent low, and slashed out in a killing arc. Ki felt the wind of the blade's passing brush his chest. He stumbled back deliberately, flailing his arms for balance. Red came after him, driving the sharp blade straight for Ki's throat. Ki ducked under the blow, spun around, and slammed his heel into Red's crotch.

Red bellowed in pain, doubled over, and backed off, lashing out with the blade to keep Ki away. He staggered, wiped his face, and bit back the pain. Anger tightened his features and the cords of his neck went rigid. Ki waited, saw muscles tighten in Red's belly, and leaped aside. Red came on relentlessly, the blade carving air only inches from Ki's eyes. Red was almost blind with the rage to kill, but some deep cunning made him wary, too careful to let Ki past his guard again.

Ki was weakening fast, and Red knew it. The beating he'd taken before had exacted its toll. Ki was dragging, his reactions a small part of a second behind the other's.

Red moved quietly, stalking Ki across the circle. Peripherally, Ki saw Cindy's blue eyes wide with pain and fear; she stared at Ki over the gag, her arms wrenched awkwardly behind her back.

Red caught his glance and grinned. "After I finish you, chink, know what I'm going to do with her? You want to hear, chink?"

Ki took a step to his left. Red followed, passing the knife easily from hand to hand. Ki waited, and Red suddenly moved. The blade thrust out, tracing a thin, shallow line from Ki's belly to his chest. He backed off, and pain tore at his side as cold metal sliced cleanly across his ribs. Ki got his footing, bent low, and landed a blow to Red's gut. Red took it without flinching and whipped the knife left and then right, a whisper away from Ki's groin. Ki leaped aside, grabbed Red's wrist, and jammed his foot behind the other's ankle. Red bellowed, found his balance just in time, and brought the butt of the knife up hard against the side of Ki's jaw.

Ki's head exploded in a burst of light. He stumbled back, caught the glint of triumph in Red's tiny eyes. The blade whipped straight for his heart, and Ki knew he was powerless to stop it. His fists came up in a last desperate motion, his body tensed to meet the pain—

The girl came up out of nowhere, ramming her head blindly at Red's belly. Red stumbled, his death blow thwarted. He took a step back, blinked in surprise, then grabbed Cindy's long amber hair in one hand and wrenched back her head.

"No!" Ki screamed, and launched himself wildly at Red. The blade sliced at the girl's neck. Ki knocked it aside and

drove both hands at Red's throat, slamming him to the dirt. Red gasped for air, pounding Ki's face with his fists. Ki held on, tightening his grip on the big man's neck. Red thrust him off his chest and slashed out with his legs. Ki blocked the blow with his knee, jabbed his fist in Red's face, and sent him reeling.

Red cried out, saw what was coming, and tried to keep his balance. He tripped over his own feet and landed squarely in the fire, sending up a shower of embers. Red shrieked and rolled away, writhing against the pain. Ki grabbed his throat again and slammed him down hard. Clutching a hot brand in his fist, he slashed it again and again at Red's face. Red howled, an unearthly sound that tore through the night. Ki stabbed out savagely, no longer aware of what he was doing. He saw Red's features through a haze of red fog, a rage that blinded him to the world. The butt of the rifle took him squarely in the head, and Ki never saw it coming...

★

Chapter 17

Jessie moved quickly through the trees, staying as close to shadow as she could. The moon was low in the sky and she guessed it was close to three. She was grateful for the light— even if it revealed her as plain as day to anyone who cared to glance up and look. At least it was better than stumbling over outlaws in the dark.

She waited a long moment, studying the small clearing. She could see the tent through the trees, smell the long-dead ashes of last evening's meal. He was sitting against a young oak, his hands bound behind him. Jessie took a deep breath and stepped cautiously into the open, long enough to let him see her before she crouched back to earth. He'd warn her now, if anyone was near. When no sign came, she moved quietly toward him on hands and knees.

Ki watched her, his dark eyes catching light from the moon. She went to her belly and eased around the tree, feeling for the ropes that held his hands. Pulling a folding knife from her pocket, she sawed through the cords. When he was free, she left him and crawled back the way she'd come, sensing him close behind her. She led him away from the camp down to the river, stopping only when she reached thick cover. He came to her then, hugged her a moment, and grinned.

"I don't guess I have to say I'm glad to see you," he told her.

"Oh, Lord, Ki—I'm so glad you're still alive! For a while I didn't— Look, we don't have much time, we've got to move fast. Are you all right? Anything broken or not working?"

Ki touched his head and flinched. "I'll make it. Jessie, what the hell happened? I don't remember a thing after fighting with Red and—" He stopped, not at all sure he wanted to ask. "Cindy . . . Jessie, is she—"

"She's all right. She's hurt some but she'll be okay. Ki, do you know that you killed Barc Hager and one of his men? You ruined Red pretty bad, burned his face something awful."

Ki clenched his fists and looked at the ground. "And I'm still alive," he said darkly. "Why, Jessie?"

"'Cause Sully came in and stopped 'em," Jessie explained. "Said if they wanted a hanging, they could by God do it when he wasn't sleeping. Sully's boys carried you off and tied you up outside his camp. I thought Barc's people were going to start a small war."

Ki looked at her. "You took an awful chance coming here."

"Uh-huh. I guess if things had been the other way around you'd have just left me to hang, right? Come on, Ki." She planted a friendly kiss on his cheek.

"And Cindy's really all right?"

Jessie let out a sigh. "I had a little luck there, I reckon. By the time Harrow and I got to where the fight was— along with everyone *else* in camp—no one was thinking about anything but stringing up the 'chink.' We got a blanket around Cindy and carried her off. They ruined all her clothes, but she fits all right in a pair of my jeans and a shirt." She sat back and looked anxiously up the hill. "This is where it gets complicated. John Harrow's asleep, but that doesn't mean he'll stay that way. Cindy's waiting in our camp. When I get back, she'll crawl off into the woods and wait. There's a big grove of trees and you'll find her in there. I haven't told her a thing, except you'll be coming to take her out." Jessie gave him a piece of a smile. "She, uh—didn't really care about why, or what *I* had to do with all this. As long as Chang was coming to get her."

"Yes, well . . ." Ki cleared his throat. "We'll make up a story of some kind for her later. The important thing is we're getting out now."

"Ki." Jessie touched his arm. "It's not exactly *we*. You and Cindy are going. I'm staying."

"What?" Ki's face clouded. "Oh, no, you're not. Just put that out of your head!"

"Listen to me," she said intently. "I got into Mattie's tent. That's what I've been trying to get away to tell you. I saw a map and I know the target. It's Austin, Ki. I don't know what they're after there, but that's close enough. Captain Simms can take it from there."

"Fine," Ki said shortly. "That makes it even better. You don't have any reason to stick around, Jessie."

"I don't want to stay, believe me. But what are they going to think if all three of us disappear? Cindy could cut you loose, and the two of you could take off. A girl freeing her man before they hang him makes sense. If *I* leave, though—I'm Cindy's friend, but I'm not even supposed to know you. I'm too close to Harrow, and he's too close to the top. Sully and Mattie wouldn't buy it. She's already got it in for me, and this would clinch it. They'd know something was wrong."

Ki shook his head adamantly. "No, I won't buy that. They aren't going to call off the raid because you took off, and you know it." He looked her straight in the eye. "The truth, Jessie. You want to stay because you still think you can unmask the cartel's agent. Look at me and tell me I'm wrong."

Jessie gave him a sheepish grin. "I never could fool you, could I? Don't know why I bother to try. All right—but that's a good reason, isn't it?"

"Not good enough to get yourself killed, no."

"Come on, I'll be fine. I am *not* going to ride into Austin with guns blazing. I'll get away before that."

"Oh, how?"

"Ki, just get Cindy out of here. Your best bet's a horse from the outriders' camp. Now I've got to get back before Harrow wakes up. Here, you might need this." She handed him the penknife she'd used to cut his bonds.

"Jessie, now listen, damn it. Jessie—!" He tried to stop her but she was already gone, vanished into the darkness along the bank.

The shots brought Jessie straight out of sleep. Harrow threw his blanket aside and sprang to his feet. "Damn it, now what!" he growled. The first hint of dawn lightened the sky. Harrow looked sleepily at Jessie, then peered at the blanket behind her. "The girl—where is she?"

Jessie turned, letting surprise show on her features. "Why, I don't know. Don't imagine she went far—she was scared plain out of her wits."

Harrow started to speak, then looked over his shoulder as Cottonmouth Sully stomped up the path, tucking in his shirt. "Sul, what's all the shooting?"

"Barc Hager's bunch," Sully said darkly. "They're madder than hell and lettin' off steam." He rested his hands on his hips and looked past Jessie. "Hager's woman is gone, huh? Don't guess I'm real surprised, considering." He fixed his eyes on Harrow. "Someone cut the chink loose. Red tried to take his bunch and go looking. I told him I'd shoot him dead if he did."

"The girl's with him, then," said Harrow.

"Oh, sure." Sully cursed under his breath. "I'm going to wish I never got into this mess 'fore it's over. Damned if I'm not!"

The morning was turning the river silver when the long column left the encampment and started north. Jessie didn't have a map, but she guessed they were more than a hundred miles south of Austin. Nearly three days under the broiling sun, if they didn't plan on killing the horses. It hadn't occurred to her before, but it began to bother her now. Did Mattie really plan to keep the gang together all the way? It didn't seem like a sound idea. There was some rough country along the way, but not that rough. They certainly couldn't avoid every small town and settlement. Why, the first person who saw close to two hundred hard-eyed men riding together would know what was up. Before the gang got anywhere close to Austin, every lawman in Texas would be sniffing them out. Lord, Ki wouldn't *need* to warn the Rangers!

And Mattie and Sully know that, too. The logical thing

132

*to do would be break the gang up, let them ride in smaller
groups—*

"You off dreaming, Sue?"

"Huh?" Jessie blinked. "Guess so. More like dozing, to
tell the truth. All that ruckus last night, and of course before
that . . ." She gave him a mischievous smile. "You sure wore
me out, Mr. Harrow. Not that I'm complaining. I—John,
what is it? What's wrong?"

He watched her with no expression at all. "Just wondering when you were goin' to tell me, Sue. Or *if* you were
at all."

"What? Tell you what, John?"

"About Cindy McGuire. And the Chinese cook."

Jessie's heart nearly stopped. Harrow let out a breath
and reined his mount close to hers. "Sue, I saw you leave
and I saw you come back. Then Cindy took off in the woods.
You let him loose, didn't you? It wasn't the girl, it was
you."

Jessie bit her lip. "Yeah, it was me."

"Why? I think maybe I've got to know that, and right
now."

"'Cause Red would kill Cindy for sure if she stayed.
You know that's so. Even if she tried to stay with us."

"And the cook?"

Jessie decided she had to look right at him. "Couple of
reasons. They—had something going between them."

"You know that?"

"Cindy told me."

"And the other reason?"

Jessie forced a smile. "You aren't going to believe that
one. I can hardly believe it myself."

"Try me," Harrow said flatly. "Damn it, Sue, this is no
joke!"

"He's—he's the one who stopped Dutch's boys from
raping me. My God, John, we stumbled right on him. He
was—relieving himself or something. One of Dutch's people pulled a knife and the cook sort of went crazy. You saw
what he did to Barc Hager and Red."

Harrow frowned thoughtfully. "All right. I can believe

133

it was the same man. Probably occurred to Sully, too. The man's no fool." He wet his lips and looked at Jessie. "Sully won't care one way or the other who the Chinaman killed, Sue. It's running off that riles him. That's not good right now, damn it."

Jessie looked at her hands. "John, those two aren't stopping to tell anyone anything. They won't slow down till they get clear to Mexico."

"You don't know that."

"I owed him, John. A life for a life. If you're mad at me, I'm sorry. I deserve it, all right?"

"Isn't quite the story you told me before."

"Yeah, I know."

"You could have let me know what you were up to," he said shortly. "After last night I thought—" He turned on her, hurt and anger in his eyes. "We've got to trust each other. You—" He stopped then and ground his heels into his mount's flanks. The horse bolted, and Harrow left her watching his back.

Before noon the column moved into low, rolling hills. There was some cover, but the country was relatively open. Too open, thought Jessie, for a small army of outlaws on the move. And in broad daylight at that. It didn't make sense, riding north in a parade. Why not simply invite the Texas Rangers to ride along with them?

She spotted Mattie once, near the head of the column. Her oversized chair was bolted firmly to the front of a flatbed wagon, a tarp stretched overhead to keep her out of the sun. She glared straight ahead, clutching the reins tightly as if they might fly away.

Later, while they were resting the horses, Jessie caught sight, briefly, of Red. His head was almost completely covered in bandages. The small part of his flesh still visible was a bright, angry crimson. Doc Holliday had told her his face was a horror—the hair all but gone and one eye gouged and burned. Jessie tried to find sympathy for the man and couldn't. What could you say about a man's getting back a good dose of what he'd handed out?

• • •

Harrow joined her again, just before dusk. He reined his mount in close, sitting stiff in the saddle. "I don't want to fight with you," he said firmly. "That's the last thing I want."

"Good, then don't," said Jessie.

"I just didn't like you lying, is all."

"Would you have helped me get Cindy away if I'd asked? Would you?"

Harrow shrugged. "I didn't stop you, did I?"

"You didn't know what I was doing, John."

"Yeah, well..."

Jessie looked at his solemn expression. Their eyes suddenly met and they both grinned at once. Harrow edged his horse up to hers and kissed her lightly on the cheek.

"I like that better," said Jessie. "Let's keep it that way, all right?"

"You've got it," said Harrow. He rode in silence a moment, then glanced over his shoulder to make sure they were alone. "You'll get the word soon, but I'm telling you now. Eat what you can in the saddle, because we won't be stopping. We'll be riding on after dark."

Jessie sat up straight. "Riding on? For how long?"

"Just stick close to me, Sue."

"Yeah, all right." His voice told her there was no use asking for more. *Now what?* she wondered. *We should have been riding in the dark in the first place, instead of marching around in plain sight...*

She tried to picture Ki and Cindy, follow their route in her head. The closest Rangers were in Gonzales, maybe fifty, sixty miles away. They'd left before dawn, and it was nearly dark now. With hard riding and maybe some luck with fresh horses, they were already there. The Rangers would telegraph the target to every lawman and army outpost they could reach. More than likely, Ki hadn't tried to make the whole trip at all. He'd stop at the first Western Union office he could find and give the Rangers extra time to get moving. If that was so, they'd been on the move half the day already; the trap was already set and ready to spring.

Jessie came erect, a sudden chill touching the base of her spine. *Lord, they could hit us any minute! Right here or over the next rise. It could happen right now!*

She didn't dare look at Harrow. If he met her eyes just then, he'd know the truth—that she'd betrayed him, maybe sent him to his death.

No, she cried out to herself, *that's not true—I won't let it happen!*

But then another voice spoke within her, asking, *What are you going to do—tell him who you are and why you're here?*

Once more she searched for an answer. And again, no answer came.

The night came quickly, closing in about the column and swallowing it up. Harrow signaled Jessie to a halt as the riders ahead slowed. "Just ride close to me," he said. "Go right where I go, Sue."

She nodded, but didn't ask why. Ahead, riders moved into a thick grove of trees, then vanished as the ground suddenly fell away to the left. Jessie leaned out in the saddle. The moon showed a creek through the trees.

In the dim light she saw the first riders reach the stream. The water eddied brightly under the horses' hooves. Jessie rode quietly at Harrow's right. There was nothing to see except the dark trunks of trees and the water. A few yards farther on, the grove thinned a little and something caught her eye. She squinted curiously through the branches. There were riders in there, bunched close together. Why? she wondered. Was Mattie holding back some of her force, while the others crossed the stream? It didn't make sense, but she knew better than to ask. Harrow had made it clear he would answer no more questions . . .

Chapter 18

The country was open, but veined with shallow ravines and a treacherous limestone surface. Ki didn't dare push the horse any faster, especially riding double. By the time the sun came up, he was certain their twisted path hadn't taken them more than ten or twelve miles from the encampment.

"We'll do better now that we can see," he told Cindy. "You doing all right?"

"I'll be fine," she said tightly, "just as soon as we're 'bout five hundred miles from that place. Lord, Chang, I ain't complaining, honest. I didn't much figure on seein' daylight this morning!"

"Neither did I," he said soberly. "It's a very pretty sunrise. The best I've ever seen."

They rode in silence, both keeping an eye on every point of the compass. Ki didn't expect pursuit—not for a Chinese cook and a girl. Still, there was no use taking chances. He tried to picture their route, and where the column might be in relation to them. He and Cindy were headed northeast, but the angle was so sharp between their path and the outlaw's route that there wasn't that much distance between them. If the column had left at first light, they could be as close as seven or eight miles southwest. *Too* close, Ki decided.

What we need are two horses, he thought to himself. One had been all he could manage without waking the off-duty guards. When the sun started blazing down in all its fury, the mount would wear out fast. He wished there were someplace safe he could leave the girl, so he could move on quickly to the nearest telegraph and get word to the

Rangers. He knew, though, that he didn't dare leave her. Not yet, not this close.

Cindy seemed to guess his thoughts. "Maybe we'll find a ranch or a farmhouse, Chang. Get us a couple of horses there."

"With what, Cindy?"

"What d'you mean, with what?"

"I mean I don't have a penny to my name. We left before payday, remember?"

Cindy laughed. "Silly. We'll get fresh horses the same way you got this one."

Ki started to speak, then decided this wasn't the time for a lecture on theft. The girl had grown up on the other side of the law. To Cindy, paying good money for something you could steal just didn't make sense.

"We'll see," he told her. "We've got to put miles behind us first. Then we'll hunt for horses."

It was close to nine when he spotted the riders. There were three of them, coming on fast from the west. Cindy saw them too, and clutched his waist hard.

"It's them," she moaned. "Oh, damn, Chang!"

"We don't know that. Hold on tight." The horse protested as Ki kicked it into a run. He took them over a rise into a thick stand of scrub, snaking the mount through tortuous twists and turns.

"I don't see 'em," Cindy shouted. "I think maybe we lost 'em!"

"Just because you can't see them doesn't mean they— Cindy, *look out!*"

Ki pitched out of the saddle, covering his face as he fell through the scrub and hit the ground hard. Wiping dirt from his cheek, he came to his feet and sprinted back to the girl.

"Cindy—you all right?"

"Yeah, just great." She picked herself up and slapped dust off her pants. "After last night, I thought there wasn't no more places to hurt. Oh, Lord, look there." She motioned over his shoulder.

Ki walked through the brush. Their horse was struggling to rise, its eyes white with fear. "Wait here," he told Cindy.

"Don't move." Running back the way they'd come, he crouched low and peered through the scrub up the hill. The riders were trotting easily along the rise. Ki cursed under his breath. Up close, it was clear they were Mexican ranch hands, minding their own business. Of all the damn luck!

Still muttering to himself, he walked back to Cindy. "It's all right," he told her. "They're not after us. We ran for nothing."

Cindy didn't answer. Ki walked back in the brush, took the folding knife that Jessie had given him, and slit the horse's throat.

The scrub gave way to open land, a fact that set Ki's nerves on edge. They were exposed, vulnerable. No money, no horse, and no weapons. In an hour the sun would be straight overhead. There wasn't a road, a ranch house, or a telegraph line in sight.

"Look, friend, I gotta stop awhile, all right?" Cindy sat down abruptly in the dirt.

Ki lifted her up. "There's shade over there. Just a little farther."

"Lord, you call that shade?"

"It's better than nothing. Come on, Cindy."

"I seen better trees in the desert," she grumbled. She left him and stomped off ahead. When he reached her she was flat on her back, a red bandanna draped over her face. "You figure there's any water nearby?"

"Somewhere, yes. I saw a line of trees to the east. Probably a creek."

"Without water in it."

"Maybe. Maybe not."

Cindy sighed and sat up. "Listen, I hate to keep complaining. But my back's hurtin' awful, Chang. Honest it is."

Ki went to her. "Cindy, I'm sorry. With everything else happening, I just—"

"I know." She kissed him lightly and Ki moved around behind her to gingerly lift her shirt. Jessie had wrapped the worst of the wounds, but the raw, ugly slashes were bleeding through. Ki knew the pain would only get worse.

139

"They're infected," he told her, "which isn't too surprising. We've got to get someone to look at you."

Cindy's eyes widened in alarm. "Hell we do. I am not stopping, Chang—not for anything but a cold drink of water!"

There was no use arguing about doctors, squatting in the middle of the brush. He helped her to her feet. "Come on, I'm as anxious for that water as you are."

It was a small dirt farm, hacked out of rocks and poor soil near the creek. There were chickens in the yard, and two sturdy mules behind the house. Ki watched the stone-and-plank house until he was sure there were only a man and his wife and a small child present.

"What you figure on doing?" Cindy said wryly. "Just ask real nice if you can borrow his animals a spell?"

"I'd like to," Ki said soberly, "but I doubt that'll work. I expect we'll have to steal them."

Cindy looked delighted. "Well, now you're talking, friend. Here's where little Cindy earns her keep." Before he could stop her, she sprang from cover and started down the draw. When Ki peered through the brush, she was staggering toward the house, holding her side.

A gaunt, middle-aged man in bib overalls came out of the house, stared at Cindy, and yelled for his wife. In a moment a dark-haired woman in a bonnet ran into the yard, and the two helped Cindy inside.

Three minutes later they were all outside again—the farmer and his wife with their hands in the air, Cindy marching behind them with an old Henry rifle.

The man's expression turned angry when Ki walked into the open. "We got nothing to take," he blurted. "You can see that plain!"

"I know you won't believe me," Ki said quietly, "but I do not intend to steal from you. We are taking your two mules and the rifle. We need food and water. If you have any money, we'll take that. In a few days I'll pay you ten times over for what we've taken."

The man stared, then laughed in Ki's face. "Don't give

140

me any shit, mister. Just don't harm the woman or my boy. I ain't askin' more than that."

Half an hour later they were headed northeast, following the trees on the far side of the creek. Besides the Henry rifle, Ki had a length of worn rope and an ax, a canteen and a flour sack of food. He'd tied the pair loosely back to back, making certain the child was safe in its bed. They'd work themselves free in less than an hour.

The farmer had watched with interest as Cindy lifted up her shirt and let the woman put salve and fresh cloths on her back. She'd caught her husband's eye, a look he'd pay for later.

"You're the most peculiar feller I ever saw, you know?" said Cindy. "Why'd you tell him all that stuff?"

"What? About paying, you mean? I said it because I meant it." He studied her a long moment. "How long do you think it took for that man to earn what we stole?"

"Hell, Chang." Cindy's blue eyes flashed. "That's his luck, not ours. Everybody takes what they can. Him included, if he ever got the chance."

"Is that what you think?"

"Think, nothing—I *know* it! You see that place they're living in? You think he wouldn't shoot you and me in the back to get out of that hole?"

"No. I don't."

"Oh, Lord." She reined up behind him, a pained look on her face. "You're strong and you're not scared of a thing, as far as I can see. But I can tell right now that I'm going to have to do the thinking for us both. If I don't, we'll sure as hell starve . . ."

Ki nearly shouted when he saw the line of poles, the telegraph wire draping between them. They followed a narrow road that snaked east through a thick stand of cedar. Reining in his mount, he sniffed the air and smelled smoke. It was the odor of burning garbage, and garbage meant a town.

"Wait here," he told Cindy. "Stay off the road. I won't be long."

Cindy stuck out her chin. "And where are you going to be?"

"There's a town down the road. It can't be far. I'm going to, uh—get some extra shells for the Henry. We haven't got enough."

"Yeah?" She leaned forward on the mule and eyed him suspiciously. "And what you using for money?"

"I don't intend to use any," he said abruptly. "You have to take what you want, remember?" He wasn't about to tell her he'd found four dollars in a bowl back at the house—plenty to do what he needed at Western Union.

Cindy brightened. "Then you better take me along, 'cause I can—"

"Forget it." Ki held up his hand and grinned. "It's a pretty small town, and you definitely attract attention. Which we don't need right now."

"Yeah, but I can steal *anything*," she protested.

Ki ignored her, turned his mule onto the road, and trotted toward the town.

It was less than half a mile through the trees, a dozen weathered buildings facing each other across the road. Ki picked out a saloon, a general store, and, halfway down the street, a Western Union office. He felt a great sense of relief at the sight. After a day that had started off badly and gotten worse, it was time for a change in his luck.

Two doors past the telegraph office was a flyspecked window with the word MARSHAL painted on it in faded gilt letters. *Good,* Ki thought. *I'll wire Gonzales—and Victoria and Austin, just to make sure. Then I'll let the marshal know what I'm up to. Not that he'll believe a story like this ...*

Swinging off the mule, he wrapped the reins around the hitch rail and stepped up on the plank porch, taking the Henry with him. Three townsmen walked out of the saloon and glanced his way. Ki turned and swung the screen door open. The room was small, no more than eight feet square. The first thing he saw was a banjo clock on the wall. It was twenty till four—he'd figured it was only one or two o'clock!

A door opened in the side of the room and a balding

142

clerk walked in, sniffing at Ki over a pair of tiny spectacles. "You want something, mister?"

"Yes," Ki said politely. "I would like to send some telegrams, please."

"Can't," the man said bluntly.

"Why not?"

"Lines are all down."

Ki gripped the edge of the counter. "But—they can't be. I have to send a message!"

"Better get yourself a pigeon, then," the man said dryly. "I ain't got any wires, and neither has anyone else."

"What do you mean?"

"Just what I said. Lines are down damn near everywhere." The clerk couldn't resist Ki's interest. "Something real peculiar going on, you ask me. I was getting in stuff from Jake Neely early this morning up at Seguin. Told me Bastrop, Austin, and Comanche had all gone dead. A minute later *he* was gone too. I started tapping out Goliad and Victoria, and on west to San Antone. Hell, they're out too. Isn't anybody sending." He paused and squinted over his spectacles. "You know anything about the telegraph business?"

"No," Ki told him, "I don't."

"Well, *I* do, boy. Having a wire down's one thing— happens all the time. Losing every damn station is something else. You know how many places you'd have to cut to do that?"

Ki didn't wait for an answer. Muttering his thanks, he turned and stalked quickly outside. He had no idea how many men the task would take, but he knew exactly who had the organization and the money to pull it off. As usual, the cartel was a good ten steps ahead of the law, covering themselves at every turn, making sure anyone who spotted the outlaw band had no way to call in help. Now he *had* to get to Gonzales, and get there fast. If he didn't, they'd—

"Just a minute, friend."

Ki stopped short. The man walking toward him wore old butternut trousers and a white shirt faded to ivory. He was edging up to sixty, but the cool gray eyes said a younger man still lived inside. The town marshal's star on his chest said the rest.

"I was coming to see you," Ki told him. "Can we talk in your office? I think I'm going to need your help badly."

The lawman almost smiled. "Well now, I need your help too. Mind if we get my problem took care of first?" He nodded toward the street without turning from Ki. "That mule belong to you, son?"

Ki tried to hide his alarm. "Yes. It's my mule. Why?"

"Mind saying where you got it?"

"No, not at all. I bought it this morning from a man south of here."

"You get his name and some paper?"

"The man's name is Ben Loving. I've got the bill of sale at my camp outside of town." Ki breathed a silent sigh of relief that he'd glanced at an envelope on Loving's table.

"You got the name right," said the marshal. "My brother Charlie sold him that mule and another like it." He scratched his stubbly jaw and looked curiously at Ki. "Funny that Ben'd do that. Sell one of the two animals he's got for plowing and riding."

Ki shrugged. "He said he needed the money. I needed a mount and didn't argue."

"Well, we can settle it simple, if you don't mind." The marshal absently hitched up his belt, his hand brushing lightly over the long-barreled Peacemaker in his belt. At the same time, his eyes flicked quickly to Ki's right. The motion betrayed him, and Ki saw the deputy in front of the store across the street. Ki moved, and the marshal went for his gun. Ki brought the barrel of his rifle up fast, knocked the lawman's hand aside, and sent the Colt spinning. The marshal stumbled back, blinking in surprise.

"Don't!" Ki bent in a crouch, whirling to face the other lawman. The young man stopped, his mouth dropping open in astonishment at Ki's speed. His pistol was in his hand, but the Henry was aimed right between his eyes. Ki wasn't about to shoot a lawman, but the deputy didn't know that.

"Drop it!" Ki snapped. "Now!" The deputy let his weapon fall. Ki collected the marshal's Colt and stuck it in his waistband, then grabbed the reins of his mule and crossed the street. Picking up the deputy's weapon, he tossed it as far as he could.

The marshal eyed him calmly. "You better think twice, boy. That mule ain't worth the trouble you're buying."

Ki didn't feel like explaining that it was. He mounted up and kicked the animal hard. Over his shoulder he saw men running out of doors and down the sunlit street after him. He urged the mule out of town and into the trees. Cindy spotted him coming and sat up straight.

"Get moving," Ki shouted without stopping. "I've got the marshal and the whole damn town on my heels!"

"Shit!" Cindy pounded her fist against her leg. "I knew I shoulda come in with you. You can't do nothing right except screw!"

Chapter 19

"Listen," Cindy demanded, "what happened back there? All you were going to do was steal some shells. Chang, honest to God—"

"Just shut up, all right?" Ki said shortly. He dug his heels into his mule's sides, urging the beast faster. "I can't stop to explain things now."

"Might as well," she said stubbornly. "We are *not* going to outrun horses on these mules."

"If you want to get down and run, go ahead."

Cindy answered with a glare. Gripping the mule's broad back between her legs, she leaned in close to the animal's neck and cursed into its ear.

"We got to do something," Cindy whispered. "We can't stay here all night. And these mosquitoes are eatin' me up!"

Ki peered out of the brush, scanning the landscape ahead. The dirt road wound by their hiding place not twenty yards away. Squinting into the afternoon sun, he saw three of the riders coming back down the hill. He recognized one as the marshal. In a moment four other men trotted back from the north to join him. *They'll look here next,* Ki decided. *The old man's doing it just right—quartering the land, keeping us bottled up.*

Each time he glanced at the sun, his gut went tight. It had to be six o'clock, maybe closer to seven.

I've got to move out. I've got to go now!

He clenched his fists in frustration. If he stepped so much as a foot out of the scrub, the marshal's posse would have him. If he stayed where he was, they'd get him almost as fast.

146

"Come on," he told Cindy, "let's get back to the mules. We're leaving here now."

"How you plannin' on that?"

"They're going to come down off that hill back to the road. They've got to look in here. While they're coming, we get out, keeping the trees between them and us."

Cindy looked appalled. "That'll just take us back the way we came!"

"Can't be helped. If we make it to cover we'll swing south. I can't see any other—" Ki stopped, took Cindy's cheeks between his hands, then clamped his palm to her brow. "God, you're burning up with fever! Why didn't you say something!" She stuck out her chin in defiance, but Ki saw the flush on her cheeks, the thin white line around her mouth.

"All right, that's it," he said firmly. "They know there are two sets of tracks, but they haven't seen you yet. I'll tie you up in here. You can tell them I stole you from a farm near Victoria. Whipped you and beat you up. They'll get you to a doctor."

"No, Chang!" Cindy clung to him, her eyes wide with fear. "Don't leave me—please. I'm scared to death of the law. I've been in jail before. I know what it's like."

"Cindy," he said gently, taking her by the shoulders, "they're not going to put you in jail."

"And you are not leaving me here," she said fiercely. "I'm going with you, and I'll—I'll be just fine."

"You'll fall off that mule," he said shortly. "Come on, damn it. I haven't got time to argue."

They mounted up quickly and rode into the open, keeping the line of trees and scrub between them. The creek with its thick stand of oaks was only a hundred yards away. If they could make it, get across the water without being spotted, there was a chance. Ki knew she was right—the mules would never outrun the horses. If he could keep ahead of them till dark, if Cindy didn't collapse...

"Come on, just a little farther," he urged her. "We're almost there."

Cindy forced a grin and bit back her pain. Ki stopped, turned around and grabbed her reins, and raced for the trees.

147

The animals whinnied in protest as he tore through the brush into the shade and thick cover. He heard Cindy gasp as he took them down the bank, plunged through shallow water and up the other side. He turned and saw her grab the mule's neck and start to sway. Her face was sallow; a slick film of moisture covered her skin.

"All right, you're stopping here, Cindy. Period."

"Chang, I'm sorry," she rasped. "I just—"

"Hold it—get your hands up fast, mister!"

Ki jerked around, startled. The two men stepped from behind tall trees, rifles steady in their hands. Ki raised his arms high, knowing at once what had happened. The old marshal was smart. He'd left two men out of the chase, roaming free and waiting for the quarry to run.

"Just drop the Henry and the Colt, real easy now," said the man to Ki's left. Ki did as he was told. Horses came through the brush behind him; he heard them splash through water, and a moment later the marshal was looking him squarely in the eye. He glanced curiously at Cindy, then turned to Ki.

"Told you it was a bad idea, son. Ain't getting any better, is it?"

"Marshal—"

"Shut up!" The lawman's weathered features went dark. "I heard all the talk from you I can stand." The man on the ground passed the Colt he'd taken from Ki up to the marshal. He scowled at it and jammed it in his belt. "First time anyone ever took a gun from me in forty years. I'm not forgetting that." He eased his horse closer to Ki. "Now you tell me, and tell it right the first time. You do any harm to Ben Loving and his folks?"

"No," Ki said evenly, "I didn't."

"Uh-huh." He studied Ki a moment, trying to guess what he saw in the almond-shaped eyes. "You better hope that's so. Get 'em on back to the road, Pete. It's getting dark out and we better—My God, what's that!"

The marshal turned in the saddle as riders appeared on the road to the right. The deputies brought their rifles up fast. The marshal raised a hand to hold them back. "Don't think you want to tangle with that bunch, Seth," he said

148

easily. "Come on, let's get these folks out of here."

A deputy gestured Ki and Cindy forward. The marshal and the rest of his men rode through the brush to the road. When Ki came out of the trees, the column of riders were off their horses, stretching and lighting up smokes. The marshal leaned out of the saddle, talking earnestly to another mounted man. He was heavyset, with a weathered face and a full white mustache. Ki glanced at him casually, then sat up straight and stared in disbelief.

"Simms!" he shouted. Ignoring the armed men at his back, Ki dug his heels in the mule and lunged forward. The marshal looked up, one hand snaking for his Colt. Simms stopped him, blinking in amazement.

"It's all right, I know this man." Simms thrust out his hand and grasped Ki's. "You are the last person I ever expected to see," he said intently. "When did you get away from 'em? Where the hell are they?"

"It's a long story, Captain. All I can say is we've got to get moving—right now."

"'Scuse me, Captain," the marshal broke in. "This boy here's in a hell of a lot of trouble. You sayin' he's one of yours?"

Simms shot him an icy stare. "Yes, marshal. Please, I don't have the time." The old man reddened and whipped his mount around. "Now. Where's Miss Starbuck? Is she all right?"

"She was when I left her. She stayed with the outlaws."

Simms shook his head. "Bad business, I'd say. And Nat Collier? Is he there too?"

Ki looked at him bleakly. "I'm sorry. Collier's dead. Clay Allison killed him."

Simms's face fell. "Jesus Christ. *The* Clay Allison?"

"Captain, I know the target," Ki said quickly. "It's Austin. I don't know specifically what they mean to hit, but that's it. They left camp this morning. I tried to get to you and ran into trouble. And all the wires are down, I guess you know that."

Simms considered his words. "Uh-huh. Austin figures. We met a rider about an hour ago—young deputy who damn near killed his horse. Said he saw the whole bunch

149

headed north—hundreds of 'em. I sent out riders to alert everyone they could. We're— Who the hell's that?"

Simms glanced past Ki, and Ki twisted on his mount. Cindy sat alone on her mule, ten yards behind him. She was staring at Ki, her eyes wide with fear. Fever flushed her cheeks, and her whole body trembled. Ki swung off his mule and ran to her side. Cindy gave a frightened cry and collapsed into his arms.

"Marshal," Ki shouted, "this girl needs a doctor. Will you get her back to town?"

The lawman looked sternly at Ki and decided the answers to his questions could wait. "Yeah, I'll see that she gets help. We got a good doc."

"Cindy, listen." He held her close, smoothing a sweat-soaked lock of hair off her brow. "I've got to leave you, but I'll be back."

"No." Cindy shook her head, nails digging desperately into his arms. "Don't—don't leave me with 'em. I—" She blinked to shake off the fever. "What's happening, Chang? I don't understand it. Lord, those men are—Texas Rangers! My God, who *are* you!"

"We'll talk about it later," he said gently. "Just rest now."

She gave a shudder and relaxed in his arms. A deputy handed Ki a canteen. Ki held it to her lips; Cindy responded to the cooling liquid, then closed her eyes with a sigh.

"We'll take care of her," said the marshal. "Just get on about your business. Only I want to talk to you again, understand?"

"Yes," said Ki. "And tell Ben Loving I meant what I said. He'll get his money's worth and then some."

"I don't think I get that."

"Just tell him" said Ki.

Ki squatted down with Captain Simms and studied the ground. A Ranger held a lantern close to the scarred earth.

"It's them, all right," growled Simms. "I'd guess more'n two hours ago, judging from the droppings. A hundred or more horses—couldn't be anyone else."

"What time is it now?" asked Ki.

Simms pulled a heavy gold watch out of his vest and

150

snapped it open. "Close on to eleven. Ten till." He brought himself erect, gave the ground a sour look, and unfolded a map in the light. "Not all of this makes a lot of sense. To my way of thinking, there's some things that just shouldn't ought to be. We're just about here." A thick finger stabbed at the map. "The Guadalupe River's still to the north. I can understand sending men to cut wire all over the country. It's a real smart move. Only it put us on the alert for something, and they must've figured that'd happen." He shook his head and frowned. "And you tell me just why they all rode out in broad daylight. Hell, they know they're going to get spotted. Why take a chance like that? They going to ride those horses all night and tomorrow, passing by folks like a Wild West show? Shit, something's not right and I don't like it."

"I agree," said Ki. "But what could be wrong? There are the tracks. Right where they should be, too. Maybe we're having a little luck for a change."

"Yeah?" Simms gave him a sour look. "I been in the law business all my life, and every time I figured I was about to get lucky, I damn near ended up dead."

At one in the morning, a Ranger reported back to Simms that a troop was coming in from north of Gonzales. Moments later the sheriff of Caldwell County rode in with twenty armed men. At one-thirty, an excited young Ranger rode back into the column, nearly getting himself shot in his haste.

"They're right ahead," he reported, "three miles up. Camped in a hollow, big as you please."

Simms frowned. "You sure it's them?"

"Yes, sir. The tracks we're trailing run straight as an arrow into their camp."

"How many guards?" asked Ki.

"None. At least not any I could see."

"What?" Simms stared at the man. "Moore!" he barked over his shoulder. "Get me the sheriff and the army feller. Let's take the bastards."

• • •

151

Ki crouched beside Simms and peered through the brush at the sleeping camp. The glow from dead fires winked in the hollow, but there was no movement at all. Simms had twenty Rangers, and the sheriff's men made up another twenty or so. Still, even with a full troop of cavalry on hand, the pursuers were heavily outnumbered. Captain Lewis of C Troop wanted to wait until dawn, but Simms wouldn't have it. There was a good moon, plenty of light to see what they were doing. Simms was counting on the element of surprise to even things up. And besides, he pointed out, there was no guarantee the outlaws would stay put until dawn. Ki had to agree. They were down now, and that was the time to hit them.

"There ought to be guards," he whispered to Simms. "That's not right. Security at the outlaw camp was first-rate, Captain."

"I *know* there ought to be guards," snapped Simms. "I don't like it any more than you do." He leaned back and angled his watch to catch the light of the moon. Turning to his left, he nodded silently to a Ranger, who slid off into the dark.

"Let's move," he told Ki. "Moore'll get 'em started."

Ki grabbed the man's shoulder. "Jessie's in there. I don't want anyone to forget that."

Simms looked at him. "You heard me pass the word," he said gently. "We'll do the best we can."

Ki didn't answer. He knew Simms's words were well meant, but didn't carry much weight under the circumstances. When the outlaws started shooting, every man there was going to empty his gun into the camp. Ki couldn't blame them for that. He knotted his fists until every muscle and tendon in his arms ached. *It's my fault she's in there—I should have dragged her out by her heels!*

The net closed as Rangers and men from the posse bellied up to the sleeping camp. The outlaws were bedded down against a thick grove of trees, and Simms had used their position to advantage. Forty men on foot formed a crescent before the camp, giving every man a clear field of fire. C Troop was mounted behind the trees. If the outlaws turned

152

to retreat through the woods, Captain Lewis's men would stop them cold.

Simms paused less than thirty yards from the camp, gave a soft whistle, and waited. In the darkness on either side, men rose to their knees and raised rifles to their shoulders.

Simms cupped his hands around his mouth and took a deep breath. "You men in the camp," he shouted clearly, "stand up slow and get your hands high. This is the law. You're surrounded, and there's no way out. I'm saying it again—try shooting and you're by God dead!"

Chaos broke out in the camp. Men jerked up out of sleep and lurched wildly about, yelling to one another. Someone fired a shot into the dark. Another emptied his rifle at the posse. Simms barked an order and the night lit up as forty rifles blazed at once, each man firing off one round after another, not two feet over the outlaws' heads.

"All right, hold it!" he yelled.

Shouts of fear went up in the camp. Every man there flung his hands in the air and shrank from the circle of guns.

"Shit," grunted Simms, "this outfit ain't all that tough. Moore, tell the troopers to come on in. We aren't going to need 'em."

Rangers and deputies moved cautiously into the camp, rifles at the ready. The men in the center backed off, all the color drained from their faces. Ki ran among them, shoving one man then another angrily aside.

"Ki," Simms bawled, "get over here pronto!"

Ki turned and pushed his way through to the Ranger. "Did you find her?" he said anxiously. "Is she all right?"

Simms's face was black with anger. He trembled with such fury that Ki started and took a step back.

"She's not here," Simms blurted, "because *no* one's here, damn it! We been sucked in like a bunch of fuckin' kids!"

"What?" Ki looked blank.

"What we have here," Simms said acidly, "is about a hundred and fifty out-of-work cowhands and drifters. Someone hired 'em last week, down south of the Nueces. They were supposed to ride north, straight up to Austin. No one told 'em why, of course. They got paid well and didn't ask."

Ki's blood ran cold as the truth hit him like a fist. "Austin's a diversion. It's not the real target. That's the map Jessie saw, and she figured that was it!"

"Uh-huh. Reckon I'd have done the same thing." Simms shook his head and squinted into the dark. "I'll bet I can put it together, and not miss it far. Remember that heavy stand of trees we passed early on, with the creek running off to the left? From the way they describe it, that's where these boys stepped into the outlaws' tracks and kept 'em moving north. The bunch we're after headed into the creek, probably keeping to midstream a long while, same way these fellers came up."

Ki's mind raced. "Back south, then? But where?"

"Southwest," Simms said soberly. "Got to be. I'll bet a year's pay those bastards hit San Antone right at dawn." The eyes that met Ki's were weary with defeat. "It's close to three now, and San Antonio's over fifty miles away. We got no way to get there in time, and no way to warn 'em with all the lines down. I told you this whole business stank. Now I know what it smells like."

Chapter 20

Jessie stood next to Harrow and watched the flatbed wagons splash through the shallows to the far side of the San Antonio River. A sparse stand of cottonwoods lined the dark water, high branches rattling in the breeze. In the haze of first light she could make out the lines of the makeshift corral, and the horses mingling inside. For the past half hour, small bands of men had been riding in hard from the east, trading their mounts for fresh ones, then disappearing quickly across the river. The change took only minutes, a shift of blankets and saddles.

Harrow had told her how it would work, late the night before when they'd turned away from the trail to the north. Jessie was grateful for the darkness that masked her expression, the cold touch of horror when she realized her mistake. The route she'd seen on the map was a diversion, the riders heading for Austin were simply hands hired to cover the trail and lead any followers astray!

"Why, though?" she'd asked, carefully choosing her words. "The law doesn't know there's going to be any raid. So what's the point of all this?"

"Because Mattie Lou doesn't miss a bet," he said evenly. "Sue, when that woman's thinkin' straight, she *knows* what she's doing. And she's right, of course. You can't keep two hundred men bottled up without someone making tracks. Mattie knew that. We think maybe at least a couple drifted off. And of course there's Cindy and your Chinese friend."

"John, I told you—those two aren't going anywhere *near* the law!"

"I don't think so either. And Jesse and Frank aren't, and not even that bastard Clay Allison. But that's the point,

155

Sue. If anyone does talk, all they know is there's a big raid somewhere."

"No one knows the target? Not even the headmen?"

"No one except me, Mattie, and Sully. 'Course, any fool could guess, seeing as how there's only one town worth anything at all the direction we're going."

"It's San Antonio, then."

Harrow grinned in the dark. "If it is, you'll know when we get there, won't you?"

Now, watching the horses and riders cross the river, Jessie knew Mattie's plan would work all too well—that she herself had unwittingly helped it along. With any luck at all, Ki had alerted every lawman in south Texas, setting them hot on the trail of the Austin raiders. And when they learned the truth it would be far too late. That was another of Mattie's tricks that Harrow had revealed: there wasn't a telegraph wire intact for more than a hundred miles around.

If I hadn't known before, I'd know it now. The cartel's hand in all this is as clear as day . . .

Harrow left her a moment, then walked back with a fresh horse. "I've got to get going," he told her, "it's about that time." He circled her waist and walked her to the edge of the river. "We're about ten miles south of San Antone, Sue. You'll go with the other women and the remounts, about fifteen miles straight west. When it's over, we all pick up fresh horses and move out on our own." He turned her to face him, holding her shoulders tight. "A lot of these damn fools will run straight for the Rio Grande. And every lawman in Texas will figure that, too. I want to cut west and then north—fifty, sixty miles up in the hill country. We can lay low there awhile, then work our way west and get a train. San Francisco, maybe. What do you think of that?"

"Yeah—that's fine," said Jessie.

His gray eyes narrowed. "Sue, you *are* with me, aren't you? Just like we talked about, that's the way it'll be. As long as it's comfortable for us both."

"Oh, God, John—" Jessie couldn't hold back the tears. She buried her head in his shoulder and Harrow held her close. "You know I'm with you. I'm just a little scared, is all."

"Don't be." He brought his lips to hers and gave her a long, lingering kiss that Jessie felt all the way to her toes. "I'll be all right. I always am." He gave her a sharp pat on the bottom and swung up into the saddle. "Next time you see me we'll be a hell of a lot richer—and *out* of the badman business."

"John—" She grasped his leg, refusing to let him go. "Listen, you don't have to do this," she said desperately. "Something could go wrong. I know you don't believe that, but it could!"

"Hey, nothing's going wrong. Don't worry. I'll be there. An hour before noon, maybe sooner than that." He touched the brim of his Stetson, then pulled his mount around and joined the others across the river. Jessie watched until he was lost among the riders.

"Goodbye," she said softly. "I know what you are, John Harrow, and that doesn't change a thing." Her eyes teared again, and the river began to blur. "Damn it all," she cried angrily, "you made me wish I was Sue Deevers, and I'm not. I'm not, and I couldn't ever be!"

Slipping away was easy.

Mattie Lou had covered every angle, but hadn't bothered herself with the outlaws' women. Why should she? thought Jessie. Their men would be back soon with their pockets full of money. The women weren't about to run off now.

There were guards keeping the remount herd in line, and outriders watching for the law. None of them paid Jessie the slightest attention when she swung down from her horse to examine the animal's leg. When the right moment came, she led the horse quietly into the trees, eased herself into the saddle, and rode off down a sandy ravine.

The first streaks of dawn were lighting the earth, and she pushed the mount hard. A mile down the dusty arroyo the trail took her back to level ground and a narrow road leading north. A lone adobe house was set well back off the road. A dog barked, and another joined in. A tall Mexican woman carrying a yoke from which hung two water buckets paused to watch Jessie pass. More buildings appeared, small adobe dwellings the color of earth or sunfaded

157

shades of rose and blue. There was a stable, a cantina, a small stone plaza.

Farther along, false-front buildings began to blend with the Mexican structures: a drygoods store, the Silver Dollar Saloon. The sky was pale yellow, but the streets were still empty, unnaturally quiet. She brought her horse to a halt, dismounted, and started knocking on every door she could find.

Where is everyone? What's happened?

Suddenly the distant sound of a bell reached her ears. Jessie stopped in her tracks. *Sunday, of course*—no wonder the town was closed up tight! In the outlaw encampment, she'd lost all track of the days. Lord, the cartel had it timed to the minute. Sunday morning at dawn, the city still asleep!

Jessie swung into the saddle and moved quickly down the deserted street. She tried to picture the town, draw a map in her head. On her previous visits she'd come in from the north, riding southwest from Austin or south from Lampasas. On a hunch she turned right, back toward the river. Three dusty streets later she veered left again. Movement caught her eye and she pressed her knees to the saddle. There was something ahead, people...

Jessie brought her mount up short, a chill touching the base of her spine. There were teams and wagons headed north into the town, canvas tarps drawn tightly over the beds. God, she'd nearly ridden right into them! She sucked in a breath, wrenched the horse around in a tight turn, and loped back the way she'd come.

It's too late. It's going to happen and I can't stop it!

A flock of chickens squawked frantically out of her path. Straight ahead, a painted sign read HOTEL. Half a dozen cowhands lounged on the porch, squinting at the morning. Jessie almost cried out with joy. Jerking back on the reins, she swung out of the saddle and ran for the porch.

"You, please—I need help!" she shouted. The men turned. One stepped off the porch, an appreciative gleam in his eye.

"Can I do something for you, miss?"

"Yes," Jessie said desperately. "I need to find the police, a constable—anyone!"

158

The man frowned. "Well, that's going to be a little hard. All the—"

His words were cut short as a sound like distant thunder shook the air. Jessie and the cowhand stared toward the north. A rapid volley of explosions followed the first—deep, rumbling sounds that shook the ground.

"Christ," the man muttered, whipping off his hat. "Look at that, will you!" Far to the north, gouts of black smoke boiled into the sky. In seconds the flat horizon was choked with heavy, churning clouds.

"My Gawd," cried a man on the porch, "the whole north end of town's blowed up!"

"Come on," shouted another, "let's go!"

The cowhands bounded off the porch, leaving Jessie standing.

"Wait, please!" she shouted after them. Men streamed out of the hotel and headed north. Jessie grasped the reins of her horse to keep the animal from bolting. She glared at the rising clouds, knowing almost at once what had happened.

It's way out of town. The wagons couldn't possibly have gotten that far.

An image of the papers in Mattie's tent flashed through her head. Dynamite—and this was what it was for, a diversion to send everyone running—*away* from the outlaws' target!

The distant clang of fire bells reached her ears. Riders, and then men on foot hurried by. Jessie grabbed a bald-headed storekeeper, forcing him to stop.

"Please," she asked him, "is there a—a bank over close to the river, or maybe a Wells, Fargo office?"

The man gave her a puzzled look. "Lady, it's Sunday—the banks are all closed. Look, I got to get up there—"

"Wait!" Jessie held on to his arm. "Just tell me, all right? Is there a bank close by—just east of here?"

"There's three of 'em," he snorted, "all in one block. Take your goddamn pick!" He shook her off and ran on, muttering under his breath.

Jessie swung onto her mount and spurred it past the hotel.

159

Two blocks farther on, she turned abruptly right, then left again. Before she reached the spot where she'd seen Mattie's wagons, she turned the horse in an alley, dismounted, and peered north up the street. Nothing. The outlaws who'd followed the wagons had already passed. Which meant they were farther north, and probably a block or so back west. She mounted again and crossed the alley quickly. Her path ended abruptly, blocked by the river that ran through the town.

A distinct, familiar odor reached her on the wind. She spurred the horse forward and found them a moment later— stockpens, hundreds of red-backed longhorn cattle milling about behind the high wooden fences. Jessie looked to her right and saw four young cowhands standing atop a chute, watching the black smoke to the north. She pulled up beside them and waved.

"Hey, can I talk to you fellows a minute?"

The men all turned at once. A towheaded youth as thin as a rail gave her a grin. "Ma'am, you can talk to me all day if you want."

The others laughed, and Jessie showed them a smile. "These cows yours, by any chance?" Her words brought another laugh from the group. "Okay, you work for the outfit that owns 'em?"

"Did," a dark-eyed boy said dully. "Till the trail boss run out of money over to Hondo and let us go."

Jessie raised an eyebrow. "You didn't get paid?"

"Not even eatin' money," the boy growled.

"Then I reckon I can help," said Jessie. "You know the Circle Star, the Starbuck outfit?"

"Yeah, sure," one of the boys answered.

"Well, that's my place and I'm hiring," Jessie said boldly.

The boys glanced at each other, then at Jessie. The dark-eyed cowhand stared. "Hell, it *is* her. I seen her once in Fort Worth!"

"It's me, all right," Jessie grinned. "You want on, I'm offering steady work as long as you like. Starting right now, and there's a year's pay bonus. Three hundred each."

The dark-eyed hand regarded her suspiciously and asked, "What in tarnation for?"

160

Jessie's face went sober. "For standing a good chance of getting shot at. You still want in?"

The towheaded boy laughed aloud. "Lady, we stand a damn good chance of starvin' to death standing here!"

Chapter 21

At first the longhorns moved reluctantly out of their pens, the leaders balking stubbornly at their new-found freedom. In moments, though, Jessie's hands had them trotting at a firm and steady pace. The riders were good, she could tell immediately. The cattle began to bawl as they picked up speed, sweeping along the flats by the river, heading north. The air was already thick and heavy with red dust.

Urging her mount ahead, Jessie rode a fast block and peered northward. Nothing. The street was empty as far as she could see.

The boy caught up and rode beside her. "Ma'am, you sure there's somethin' going on here? Sure seems quiet."

Jessie didn't answer. She quickened her pace, warning the young man back. Guiding her horse cautiously to the corner, she risked a quick look. The sight sent her scurrying back to cover. There they were—overturned wagons blocking both ends of the street, horses and riders mingling about in between.

"It's them," she told the boy shakily. "It's happening right now!"

"How many, can you tell?"

"I don't know. There are close to two hundred in the whole gang. Depends on how many are blowing up the north end of town. Come on, we've got to get moving. You're Jack, right?"

"Jack Hawker." The boy's face suddenly went slack. "Christ A'mighty. Two hundred outlaws?"

"I told you," Jessie said dryly. "You and your friends just didn't believe me." She laid a hand on the boy's arm.

"Jack, I meant what I said. I hired you to drive cattle and that's all."

Jack forced a grin. "Hell, Miss Starbuck, I don't aim to buy me a pine box with that money." He spurred his mount, loped back up the street, and gave a shrill whistle. His friend two blocks away waved his hat and turned back to the herd. In a moment the cattle were thundering down the street, two hands bringing up the rear, the other pair on point, funneling the rangy beasts toward Jessie. At a signal from Jack, his companion dug in his heels and crossed his mount ahead of the herd. The two began to yell and beat their hats against their legs, forcing the cattle to the right.

Jessie sucked in a breath. For an agonizing moment the herd refused to turn. Tons of sharp horn and stringy meat rolled straight for the two young men, giving no sign of stopping. Jack and his friend stood their ground, waving their arms and swearing like demons. At the last instant the lead animals dug their hooves into the ground, rolled their eyes, and veered sharply to the right.

The cowhands cheered; the pair at the rear drew their pistols and fired into the air. Panic swept through the red-backed mass as the cattle suddenly lurched forward. At the inner angle of the turn, animals bunched up in confusion and bounded clumsily over the boardwalk, driving through windows and splintering the wooden storefronts with their weight.

A shout went up from the wagons, lost in the noise of the fear-stricken herd. Jessie frantically waved the cowhands to cover as outlaws emptied their rifles at the cattle bearing down upon them. The front of the herd balked and tried desperately to turn away, but the animals behind drove them on. Through a choking cloud of dust, Jessie saw the cattle thunder headlong into the overturned wagons. Wood split and a wheel flew into the air. Men yelled and ran for cover as the herd poured into their midst. Horses and pack animals added to the chaos, bolting before the herd and running men down in the street. In the span of a few seconds, fleeing outlaws, terrified mounts, and the leading edge of the long-horn stampede reached the second pair of overturned wag-ons. The first men to reach the barriers clambered over the sides and leaped to safety. Horses shrieked and threw their bodies against the wall. One of the wagons shuddered and moved a good six feet down the street.

The herd had lost its momentum and the mass began to turn back on itself. Wild-eyed steers shook their heads and bawled, circling blindly through the dust. Jessie stared astonished at the chaos she'd caused. Now outlaws were streaming out of doorways, dodging wicked horns to run down their mounts. Jessie saw two men reach a horse at once. The first swung into the saddle, a bulging canvas bag over his shoulder. The second drew his gun, fired once at the rider's chest, and pulled him out of the saddle.

Jack urgently grabbed Jessie's arm. "Lady, this'd be a damn fine time for us to sorta leave, don't you think?"

"We've slowed them down," said Jessie, "but this won't stop them."

Jack stared. "Miss Starbuck, I don't know if you noticed, but we're fresh out of cattle. Far as I'm—oh, *shit!*"

Jessie saw them out of the corner of her eye. Jack grabbed her reins and jerked her horse roughly to cover. A dozen outlaws whipped past them, spurring their mounts south. They bent low to their horses, none stopping to glance to either side.

"Henry," Jack shouted over his shoulder, "where's Ezra and Blake?"

Henry gestured past Jessie. The two young men who'd brought up the rear were wisely keeping to cover on the other side of the street. Jack caught their attention and motioned them toward the river.

"Best thing for us is to circle back west," he told Jessie. "Come on, I ain't at all comfortable here."

Before Jessie could answer, gunfire suddenly erupted from the far end of the street. The first quick shots were answered by a withering volley of fire, a sound that rolled like a flat clap of thunder off the false-fronted buildings.

"Hey," Jessie cried, "maybe we've got some help at last!"

"Maybe," Jack said dryly. "You want to wait around and find out?"

The gunfire came again—quick, sporadic bursts, then a

steady answering fire. Jessie glanced to the north. The smoke from the explosions was only a thin gray pall drifting over the city. Jack brought his horse up short, nearly causing Jessie to collide with him as the four riders bolted around the corner from the east. Jack reached for his Colt, but quickly decided against it.

"Good idea, son." The stocky man in front of them turned his mount in a half circle, leveling his rifle at Jack. "Who are you two, and what the hell are you doing here?"

Jessie's alarm turned to relief as she saw the bright star on the man's chest. "Listen," she said anxiously, "about a hundred outlaws are robbing the bank up there—maybe *all* the banks, I don't know!"

The lawman screwed up his face. "Lady, don't you think I know that? Jed—get these two out of here somewhere. I want to see 'em later."

"Wait," Jessie shouted, "I've got to talk to you, damn it!"

The lawman turned away as a dozen armed riders brought their horses to a halt just behind him. He barked out orders and they swung off their horses; half ran into the alley while the others took up positions at the corner. One peered cautiously up the street, then motioned the others forward. The men went to their knees and began emptying their rifles toward the wagons. The outlaws answered their fire and the men scattered for cover.

A lone longhorn steer trotted around the corner, rolled its eyes, and scampered off toward the river. A dozen more followed, then a steady stream of cattle poured into the street.

"Come on, you two," snapped the deputy. "Get on back out of the way and sit tight. And *be* there when old Kirby wants to see you." He waved them off and trotted back to find his boss.

Jessie glared and clenched her fists. "Damn it, I've got to talk to someone. They don't understand what's happening!"

"What we've got to do is get out of here," Jack said anxiously. "Me and the boys'd just as soon be somewhere

165

else when that lawman starts askin' about them cows."

"Jack," Jessie told him, "I'll take care of that, all right? Right now I—"

A violent explosion cut off her words. Jack shouted something she couldn't hear, bent to the saddle, and drove his mount off the street into the alley. Jessie followed, reaching cover as one shattering explosion followed another. Jack dragged her off her horse and threw her to the ground. The building behind them shook as shards of glass and burning wood rattled on the roof. Jessie risked a look as a geyser of red dust erupted in the street, pelting them with dirt and small stones.

"Hell!" shouted Jack. "What's going on out there!"

"Dynamite," snapped Jessie, clamping her hands tightly over her ears. "They didn't use all of it north of town."

"Hey, where you think you're going?"

"Nowhere," she told him, "just want to take a look." Keeping low, Jessie moved to the mouth of the alley. Several lawmen lay still in the street. Longhorns loped through the dust, heads hunched low and bawling with fear. A man shouted somewhere as a dark bundle arched over the street. Jessie ducked as the blast shook the air. A storefront exploded across the way. Black gouts of smoke rolled out of the building. Jessie heard a scattering of shots. A man screamed and four lawmen sprinted for cover. One stopped to fire, dropped his weapon, and sagged to the dirt.

"Ern, Lester!" a man bawled. "Get your boys up here, they're coming out!"

Men rushed past Jessie, heading for the corner on the run. Suddenly a withering volley of fire came from the street to her left. Riders thundered into the crossing, emptying their guns at the lawmen, spurring their mounts south. Hard on the tail of the riders came a team of white-eyed horses pulling a flatbed wagon. Jessie shrank back as she recognized Mattie's hulking shape at the reins. Before the wagon disappeared, she caught a glimpse of Cottonmouth Sully. He gripped the bed of the wagon, his features twisted in pain, dark blood staining his shirt.

For a moment the street went silent. A short burst of gunfire echoed from the other end of the street. Jessie guessed more of the outlaws were breaking out to the north. She wiped dust off her face as dazed men picked themselves up and staggered to cover. She saw the heavyset lawman come to his feet and check his rifle. Another outbreak of gunfire reached Jessie's ears, this time from farther away.

"Some of 'em got out the other end," said Jack. "Trying to make it to the river."

Get away safe, Jessie said silently. *Get away, John!*

"Ma'am, something wrong?"

"No. I'm fine, Jack."

"The horses spooked off up the alley. Stay right here and I'll look."

"Yes, all right." She stared at the nearly empty street, listening to the gunfire to the east.

"Listen," Jack spoke angrily behind her, "you fellers just— Jesus, *don't!*"

Jessie jerked around and went rigid. Jack staggered back and fell, his hands clutching his head. The riders came out of nowhere, rounding the curve of the alley. Jessie tried to run but the man was already on her, his big stallion forcing her to the wall. He leaned out of the saddle, grabbed her under the arms, and wrenched her off the ground. A scream died in her throat as a dark hand covered her mouth. The face she could no longer see left an afterimage burning in her mind—the scarred, twisted features as bright as fire, the terrible empty eye...

Chapter 22

The riders came to a halt as white light rippled against the dull morning sky. In seconds the sound reached their ears—the muted roll of thunder, the burst of distant cannon.

"Look there, to the northwest!" The young cavalry officer bulled his lathered mount between Ki and Captain Simms. The faraway explosions came again, and this time Ki saw plumes of black smoke smudge the sky.

Simms cursed under his breath. "That's San Antone, north of the city. Shit—we're too damn late!"

"What's up there?" asked Ki. "What could they hit?"

"Don't know the place that well. Could be anything." He turned to Captain Lewis. "You got better mounts, so why don't you head up north? I'll take my boys and half the sheriff's men, cross the river below town, and head back up. Some of the bastards will break south. Maybe we'll be there if they do."

The officer nodded, touched his hat brim, and shouted at his sergeant.

Simms looked at Ki and read his expression. "She'll likely be all right. Looked to me like a lady who can take care of herself."

Ki didn't answer. He urged his mount down the shallow hill, his eyes on the black smoke rising ahead. Behind him, harnesses rattled as Captain Lewis's troopers took off in a trot. Ki's horse stumbled and blew air, weary and ready to drop. On a map, it was a straight line sixty miles back to where they'd found the decoy riders. In the dark, though, over rough country, it was a hell of a lot farther than that. Each man had taken an extra mount from the bunch they'd rounded up, but men and animals were dead on their feet.

"You can go with them if you like," said Simms. "I figure we'll have better luck, though."

Ki looked over his shoulder at the bleary-eyed Ranger. "I think you're right. They'll go south if they can."

Simms laughed in his throat. "Damn outlaw'll run for Mexico like it was his mama. Do it every time."

They were still a mile from the river when they heard the shooting start. Ki stopped and stood up in the saddle. "That wasn't north. It's a lot closer than that."

A grin creased Simms's weathered features. "What did I tell you? And someone's giving 'em a fight, too. Harris, Parker! Take three men and get over that river. Get word back to me fast!"

Simms waved his column into a run, following on the heels of his scouts. In moments they were past the muddy shallows and into the outskirts of town. Men passed them on horseback and on foot, hurrying toward the gunfire to the north. Suddenly a loud explosion ripped the morning air, then another and another. Ki's horse tried to dance in a circle. He cursed it, brought the reins back hard.

"Not far," snapped Simms. "Four or five blocks at the best. We'll be— Christ, now what's *that* doin' here?"

A rangy longhorn loped down the street, stared at the Rangers, then lurched off to the west. Seconds later a dozen more went by, running scared.

A Ranger shouted a warning, gesturing rapidly to the north. Ki heard pounding hooves and a scattering of gunfire seconds before the outlaws burst out of the street just ahead, emptying their weapons at the Rangers. Simms's men braced their knees against their saddles, jerked their rifles up fast, and answered the outlaws' fire. The riders streaked by, forty or fifty men bent low, firing blindly at whatever lay in their path. A haze of red dust choked the street. Ki pulled his horse aside as a flatbed wagon thundered out of the dust on the heels of the riders. He only glimpsed the driver a moment, but knew it was Mattie Lou.

"Captain, on the wagon—that's the one we want!" he shouted.

Simms squinted up the street. "Davis—take six men and see what else is coming. The rest of you get those bastards!"

169

The Rangers turned their horses and raised dust southward. Ki hesitated, glancing back the way the outlaws had come. Where the hell was Jessie? Not with the raiders, she had more sense than that. The truth suddenly struck him and he whipped his mount after the others. The outlaws were heading back south, trying to break free. He knew Jessie well, and guessed what she'd do. Harrow would leave her somewhere safe—only Jessie wouldn't stay there, she'd get away and try to alert the law to the raiders' plans.

"Jessie, Jessie," he muttered to himself, "stay out of trouble, damn it, just this once."

The sound of gunfire guided him down the street. Simms spotted him and waved him down. The captain was hunched up behind an adobe wall, fifty yards from the river. The Rangers' horses were gathered under a tree; the men poured a steady barrage over the wall.

"They're holed up in that big tin shack," Simms told him. "'Bout thirty of 'em, I guess. Bunch of my boys east of the shooting got smart, rode back here and cut them off. Got three windows to fire through, but it isn't going to do 'em much good."

"Is the wagon there?"

Simms nodded. "Threw a wheel and hit a tree. If those boys hadn't stopped to help, we'd likely have lost them."

Ki squinted past the wall. "They didn't come back to help Mattie. That means the money's there, Captain. Or whatever it is they got."

Simms nodded. "Yeah, that figures." He brought himself erect and checked the chambers of his Colt. "All right, let's button this business up." He talked a long moment with two of his men, then walked to his horse, pulled a Winchester free, and handed it to Ki.

"You told me you aren't too fond of firearms, but I'm real itchy about keeping my ass covered. If you're going with me, you hang on to that."

Ki took the rifle but shook his head. "Jessie's around here somewhere. I've got to find her."

"Somewhere's right," said Simms. "You want my advice? All you're going to do is a lot of riding. I know that seems

170

like a good idea but it's not. Stick with me another ten minutes and I'll give you a bunch of fellers happy to answer questions. Find out where they were going to get fresh horses."

"She wouldn't stay put, Captain."

"I know that," Simms said impatiently, "but it'll give us a start, all right? And I can free up some men to ride with you."

Ki didn't like it, but he knew Simms's suggestion was sound. Racing all around San Antonio and half of South Texas wouldn't help. "All right," he said reluctantly. "But I want to talk to one of those bastards fast."

"Fast as I can get you one," Simms promised. He went to his horse again, threw a leather satchel over his shoulder, and spoke to one of his men. Moments later, half of the Rangers poured a steady volley into the shack while the others moved up. Then the forward squad picked up the chore, peppering the tin wall with lead.

Simms waved a hand and the guns went silent. "You inside," he shouted, "I am Captain Horace T. Simms of the Texas Rangers. Back out one at a time with your hands up high. You'll get a fair trial. You got twenty seconds."

Simms pulled out his big gold watch, counted off the time, and shut the case. Slipping it in his pocket, he reached into the satchel and pulled out a tight bundle. Ki blinked in surprise. Somewhere Simms had picked up some of the outlaws' explosives. As Ki watched, the captain chose a stick and lit the fuse with a sulfur match. The fuse began to spit sparks, and Simms walked calmly up on the blind side of the shack, jammed the dynamite under the wall, and took off running.

A bare second after he stepped behind a tree, the dynamite went off. There was a deafening roar and a quick flash of light. The building shuddered and a sheet of tin blew twenty feet into the yard. Outlaws poured out of the hole, waving their arms and choking on dust. Rangers herded them outside and shoved them to the ground facedown.

Ki picked his man and took him aside. It took only a moment to get an answer to his question. Yes, there was a point a few miles to the south where fresh mounts were waiting. The women had stayed there too, if they were still hanging around.

"Jessie's not here," Ki muttered to himself as he walked away from the building. "Damn it, I'm wasting time here!"

"Ki," Simms called out, "hold on there!" Ki turned and Simms walked toward him, worry creasing his brow. "That woman, the fat one. She's not inside."

"What? But the wagon—"

"I know the wagon's there. The woman's gone, I'm telling you."

"That doesn't make sense. She was—"

The dull, throaty roar of a shotgun cut off his words. Ki stared at Simms, then broke into a run, clutching the rifle in his fist. The wagon was on the other side of the shack, one end tilted up at an awkward angle. He squatted down and saw where Mattie Lou had crawled through the grass after hiding next to the broken wheel.

"Damn," Simms cursed. "She never was in the building at all."

"Captain, over here!"

Ki and Simms stepped quickly through the trees, knowing already what they'd find. A Ranger was sprawled on his belly, his body cut nearly in half. Rifle fire sounded by the river, and Ki ran ahead, leaving Simms behind. He saw her almost at once, waddling through the cottonwood grove like a bear, bullets from Ranger rifles churning up dirt at her heels.

"Hold it!" Ki shouted. "We don't want her dead!" He cut to the left toward the river, Simms right behind him. Mattie Lou came out of the trees, thirty yards ahead. At first Ki thought she'd somehow doubled her weight, grown even more enormous. Then the illusion vanished and he saw that she was burdened with canvas bags, bulging sacks slung over her shoulders and clutched in her arms.

Ki stared, unable to take his eyes off the sight. At that instant a pair of Rangers broke through the trees to Mattie's right. Mattie heard them. She turned, her eyes bright with cunning and fear.

"Lady," Simms called out, "you can stop right there.

There's no place to go and you know it."

Mattie didn't answer. She waddled down the bank and into the river, ignoring the rifles at her back. The river was shallow there, the current slowed by a stretch of flat stones. Without looking back, she placed one stubby leg before the other, calmly making her way through the water.

"Christ." Simms made a painful noise in his throat. "What in all hell does she think she's doing? Davis, get that woman up here right now!"

A young Ranger handed his rifle to his companion and stalked toward the water. Mattie suddenly turned, apparently sensing he was there. Ki saw it—the dull glint of the sawed-off shotgun barrel, the stock cut to a pistol grip, the twin barrels scarcely a foot long . . .

"Davis,—*look out!*" he shouted. Mattie brought her hand up fast. The Ranger froze and threw himself aside. The weapon roared with a bright flash of orange. Shot grazed the boy's sleeve and shredded leaves at his back. Mattie teetered and let out a cry as the kick of the weapon drove her back. The canvas sacks went flying and she hit the water hard, sending up a huge splash. She disappeared for a second, then came up gasping, flailing the water with her hands. Suddenly the tight yellow curls slipped off her head and floated away, revealing a bald pate as slick as a melon. A few of the Rangers laughed. Simms quieted them with a look.

"Go on, get her out of there," he said sharply.

Two men waded into the water and started toward Mattie. The current was slow, the water barely up to her neck, and the Rangers took their time getting to her. The canvas bags bubbled up like pillows full of air. She eyed the men with cold anger, paddling her arms in the water.

Ki watched, wondering if he was dreaming the whole thing. The cottonwoods stirred in the breeze and the sun sparkled on the river. Mattie Lou didn't belong there at all. She ruined the pleasant scene, made it seem all wrong.

"Damn it," Simms suddenly exploded. "Get her out, fast!"

Ki blinked, stared at Mattie Lou, and saw her face go dark, her pale eyes widen with fright. A strangled cry caught in her throat; her arms clawed the air, fighting an enemy no one could see. In a second she was gone, her head lost under the surface. The Rangers swam toward her, clothes and boots dragging them back. One of the bags she'd been carrying popped to the surface. As Ki watched, sodden greenbacks spilled from the bag and floated on the water.

A Ranger went under, surfaced quickly, and shouted at Simms. "I can't find her, Captain—she's drifted off somewhere!" The other man slid beneath the water, came up for breath, and dove once more. When he popped up again, he cupped his hands and yelled to the shore, "Get a rope or something! I've got her!"

They stood around her, none of them talking, but only watching as the water drained off her body and darkened the earth. It had all been so quick, so unexpected, they still couldn't believe it had happened. One of the Rangers pried Mattie's clenched hands from her throat. Her eyes were wide and staring, her face purple. When her hands came away, the men standing about shook their heads. They could see at once what had happened. The sacks of paper money had helped keep her afloat before they'd started to fill with water. There were eight sacks in all, bound together in pairs with leather straps. Ki had seen guards carry them into banks that way over their shoulders. Cords from several sacks had become twisted around her neck. She'd struggled, panicked, and tried to tear them loose. The leather was bound tight about her throat. A Ranger had to cut the straps with his knife.

"She didn't drown at all," Simms said almost to himself. "Hell, she didn't have time."

Ki stared at the still figure, the gown clinging wetly to the mountain of flesh. With the yellow wig gone and the shaven head showing, Mattie looked obscenely naked.

"I've got to get moving," said Ki.

"Yeah, all right." Simms stood with his hands jammed in his pockets.

"Christ A'mighty, Captain!" The young Ranger straightening the tangled gown over Mattie's thighs suddenly dropped the wet cloth like a brand and jumped to his feet.

174

"What's wrong with you?" asked Simms.

"Sir—" The boy swallowed and looked as if he might be sick. "That—that thing ain't a *she* at all, Captain. I'm not sure what the hell it is, but it ain't a *he* either!"

Ki walked back through the trees past the ruined tin shack, crossed the dusty road to the adobe wall and the horses. Jessie wouldn't be where the outlaw had said. She wouldn't stay with the mounts, she'd get herself away as soon as she could.

He grasped the pommel of the saddle, placed his foot in the stirrup. Suddenly every muscle in his body went rigid. He looked up slowly, over the back of the horse, knowing before his eyes met the other man's that he was there.

Red stepped from behind the tree, his Colt leveled straight at Ki's head. At first Ki saw nothing but the ruined face, the barrellike chest. Then, from the corner of his eye he saw her, her wrists crushed cruelly in Red's massive fist. Ki's blood ran cold. Red jerked her roughly to her feet, clamping Jessie's throat in the crook of his elbow.

Red looked at Ki and grinned, the motion twisting his features into a horror. "I seen you with them lawmen, Chink." His mouth stretched into a snarl. "Clyde and Wooter said I was crazy to hang around, but I told them that gettin' *you*, by God, was worth the damn risk!" He motioned to Ki with the gun. "Move away from that horse so I can see you."

Ki did as he was told. Red watched him, a terrible gleam in his single beady eye. "You got Cindy," he said flatly. "Where is she?"

"Cindy's safe. Where you can't touch her."

"Damn you!" The barrel of the Colt shook as Red's fingers tightened on the trigger. "Where is she!" he raged.

"I told you," Ki said calmly. "You'll never see her again, never hurt her, Red."

Red almost choked on his fury. He ground his teeth and let out a breath. "Don't even need the little slut no more. I got me another pretty."

Ki didn't dare meet Jessie's eyes. "That's your business, not mine. She's Harrow's woman."

"She's also the bitch that let you an' Cindy loose," barked

175

Red. "I got a good idea she's the one!" He jammed the muzzle of his pistol against Jessie's throat. Jessie gasped and closed her eyes. "When I finish playin' with her, she's goin' to tell me all about that. Ain't you, pretty lady?"

Ki shook his head. "The woman is Cindy's friend, but she didn't let me go. Cindy did that."

"You're lying, damn you!"

Ki shot him an easy grin. "You can't think about it, can you, Red? Cindy's beaten you, and Barc Hager and all the others."

"Shut up!" Red straightened his arm, threatening Ki with the pistol.

"Kill me," Ki said flatly. "There are more Texas Rangers down by the river than you'd ever hope to see. What do you think they'll do when they hear the shot?" Ki laughed aloud. "You're as crazy as your friends said you were. Standing here ready to die for a Chinaman—and a girl you can't touch!"

A terrible sound came from Red's massive chest. In one motion he tossed Jessie roughly aside and leveled the Colt at Ki's head.

Ki was already moving, the balls of his feet launching him off the ground. He turned his head to the right as the shot exploded, the hot muzzle flash singeing his hair. His head caught Red full in the chest; air spilled out of the man's lungs and he hit the ground hard. The gun flew away as Ki rolled, leaping to his feet. Red's heavy boot lashed out and smashed into his thigh.

Ki staggered and caught himself as Red came at him from the ground, big fists churning like pistons. Ki took the blows, twisted from Red's killing grasp, and whipped the hard edge of his palm at the base of Red's neck. Red grunted, shook his head, and stumbled back, trying to get his bearings. Ki came in low, his fingers bent like claws. Red jabbed with his right. Ki ducked and came in close, lashing Red's face with two wicked blows, then dancing clear before the other could blink.

Red wobbled, bunched the muscles in his shoulders, and spat blood. Ki waited, letting the man stalk him, remem-

ering the moment in the clearing when Red had come after
im with the whip. Red feinted with his left, shifted his
ance, then brought his right up hard. The fist stung the
de of Ki's face and drew blood. He leaped back, spun in
full circle, and hit Red solidly in the chest with his foot.
ed took the blow, grabbed Ki's leg, and jerked him off
is feet. Ki yelped in surprise, the man's incredibly fast
action catching him completely off guard. Red slammed
im viciously to the earth, the blow stunning every nerve
Ki's body. Gritting his teeth against the pain, he wrenched
imself free and rolled desperately from under Red's boot,
hich was coming down fast to stomp him.

Pulling himself erect, he heard Jessie's warning—but it
as too late, his head slammed hard against the trunk of a
ee. Red laughed aloud and came at Ki with both big hands
pread wide, ready to choke his life away. For an agonizing
cond Ki felt the brutal fingers at his throat, saw Red's
rrible features close to his own. Darkness clouded his
ision as he brought his fists together, then drove them
raight up with every ounce of his strength.

The blow took Red full on the chin, snapping his head
ack and sending him reeling. Ki gasped for breath and
ame at Red in a crouch. He drove one blow after another
ito the big man's face. Red tried to throw up his arms, but
i came on relentlessly, breaking bone and cartilage. He
w the man's face through a red film of rage, watched him
agger helplessly from one deadly blow after another...

Ki stopped suddenly, shrinking back in horror, nauseated
the anger that surged through his veins. He stepped away
nd let Red fall limply to the ground. He had come too
lose—he'd almost let the man poison him with his own
y of death...

Red groaned, tried to bring his hands up to his face, then
ll back and lay still. Ki stepped over him and walked back
Jessie. She came to him and wrapped her arms tightly
out him.

"I'm real glad to see you, old friend. Oh, *Ki!*"

Ki gave her a weary smile. "You can't stay out of trouble,
an you? Why did I imagine that you could?"

Jessie didn't answer. "I found the pistol, but I was afraid to use it, afraid I'd hit you instead."

"That's all right," he told her, guiding her back to the horses. "It ended the way it needed to end..."

Chapter 23

aptain Simms stood, set down his glass, and smiled at
:ssie and Ki. "I'm obliged for the brandy, Miss Starbuck.
hat went down good."

"I'm glad you could come, Captain," said Jessie. "I ap-
reciate your thinking of me."

"Well," he said gruffly, "You, uh—played a big part in
.is business. Figured you had a right to know how it came
ut." He started for the door and then turned. "Oh. Almost
orgot. Looks like we're going to end up with about seventy-
ve or eighty fellers going to prison. There's around twenty-
ve dead, and a couple hurt bad." His lips curled as if he'd
.ddenly discovered a bad taste in his mouth. "Means maybe
hundred of 'em still running loose. Don't much care for
.at."

"I think you did a real fine job," said Jessie.

"Yeah, well, we're not finished yet." He looked thought-
.lly at Jessie. "That, uh—foreign cartel business you talked
bout in Galveston—"

"Yes, Captain?"

"I know Nat Collier found that piece of paper and set
ou thinking. And I'm not denyin' you saw a—symbol or
omething. Only thing is, Miss Starbuck, as far as anything
e've been able to dig up, there's nothing else here 'cept a
amn clever plan to empty banks." Simms cleared his throat
nd looked away. "That woman who wasn't a woman was
ehind the whole thing. Everybody we caught says that.
iot a record in California and a couple of other places."

Jessie smiled. "You're probably right, Captain. Maybe
.at's all it was. As you say, a very well organized plan to
ob banks."

179

"Well, I'll be seeing you folks, then." He touched h[is] hat, and Ki walked the lawman to the door and let him ou[t.] Turning back into the room, he let out a sigh and ran a ha[nd] through his hair.

"I missed the first of all that. Did he say anything else[?]"

"About what you'd expect. Did you get your wire?"

Ki grinned. "Cindy's doing fine. The marshal says t[he] doctor reports she'll be up and around in no time."

Jessie pretended to study her hands. "We'll be getti[ng] the train back to Austin in the morning. Maybe you oug[ht] to stop off along the way and ride over to see her. You'[ve] got to talk to that marshal, of course, and pay off our de[bt] to the owner of those mules."

"Yes," Ki said soberly, "that's true. I should take ca[re] of that."

Jessie walked to the hotel window and looked down [at] the streets of San Antonio below. It was close to no[on] already, and she found it hard to believe they'd been [in] town only a short day and a half.

"I had a visitor while you were gone," she told Ki, turni[ng] back into the room. "Mort Wheeler, who looks after t[he] Starbuck cattle interests here, and a couple of other thing[s.] He's been on the wire to Arthur Lewis in San Francisc[o.] You remember him, of course."

"Yes, I remember." Ki knew that Lewis looked af[ter] Starbuck imports and exports in California, but that he al[so] handled a good deal more than that. Where Jessie's intere[sts] were concerned, he was a gold mine of information, diggi[ng] up a great deal that the law couldn't find, or sometim[es] chose to ignore.

"Arthur must have kept his sources running all nigh[t,]" Jessie reported. "Mattie Lou's operation is no secret [up] there, but Arthur did some prying and took it back furth[er.] Mattie was a he, of course—a eunuch. Nobody knows h[ow] he got that way, but Arthur thinks it happened in Pers[ia.] His sources think Mattie was the son of a Prussian diplo[mat] stationed in that country. As a young man, this 'Matt[ie'] went by the name of Farhad, and maybe helped the Russia[ns] get a foothold in northern Persia. Later, back in Europe,

180

was known as Frederick Saxe. Whoever he was, he was just as mad as we figured, and ten times as dangerous and cunning. He very definitely worked for the cartel, Ki. Arthur is certain of that. A suspect resembling this Frederick Saxe was linked to Emil Hödel a couple of years back—and Hödel tried to kill Kaiser Wilhelm."

Ki bit his lip in thought. "Guess he figured out the female disguise when the cartel sent him over here. The kind of people he'd have to deal with would laugh at a castrated man, but they'd accept an overweight woman—especially if she proved what she could do."

Jessie nodded, and Ki caught the gleam in her eye. "Mort Wheeler's been busy too, Ki. The outlaws robbed three banks yesterday—but only one had what Mattie was after. About a million dollars in cash."

Ki raised an eyebrow at that.

"They would have gotten it too, if our—uh, cattle drive hadn't worked out, and you and your friends hadn't come along when you did."

"And the other banks were just feints?"

"Sort of. There was money in them, but not much. Mattie'd told her gang that all three banks were overflowing with money, so that she—or he, or it, whatever—could field a force large enough to divert attention from her real objective. Obviously she intended to keep the proceeds from *that* one to herself. She figured to get away in all the confusion and leave the gang to face whatever music there might be. As things worked out, though, she only got about seventy-five thousand, and nearly all of that has been recovered from the river."

Ki looked at her a long moment. "That's not all of it, though, is it?"

"No," said Jessie, "it's not." She filled her glass and Ki's with amber brandy. "This is the part Wheeler says will likely never come out. The money in that bank was slated for investment in Mexican railroads. The Mexicans insisted the money be delivered in cash. The cartel found out. They wanted the Mexican deal, but other investors beat them out. So they figured a way to get what they wanted. Rob the bank and ruin the investors, then step in and take over the deal. They'd also get the cash, and the robbery would likely destroy the bank's reputation."

"And the cartel's men step in and get themselves a bank for next to nothing, as well," Ki finished.

Jessie stood and faced the window again. "Mattie probably didn't even know that end of the deal. That's the way the cartel works. It's like those little Chinese boxes—you open up one box and find another inside. And another inside that. Lord, Ki—" She turned to him, and he saw the touch of anguish in her eyes. "We beat them sometimes, but we never beat them enough!"

"We will," he said softly. "We will, Jessie."

The clock in the hotel lobby said seven when she walked outside and turned south. The air was still sultry and heavy, but cool shadows stretched over the streets. Jessie quickened her steps, crushing the folded paper in her fist. The young Mexican boy had knocked on her door, handed her the note, and then vanished. The few words written there had shaken her, made her legs as weak as water and brought a cry of relief to her lips.

Now she wasn't at all sure she'd made the right choice. He was all right—that was what counted. Seeing him again, though—She cast the thought aside. *God, Jessie, what are you thinking about? Of course you're going to see him!*

The cantina was dark and cool. Two Mexicans sat at a table in the corner. They glanced up curiously at Jessie, then looked back into their drinks. The bartender caught her eye, and nodded over his shoulder. Jessie walked through a beaded curtain, down a narrow hall, and into a small, whitewashed room.

Harrow stood as she entered, looked at her with no expression at all, then took her into his arms. He kissed her soundly, then held her away. "I wasn't sure you'd come."

Jessie's green eyes didn't waver. "Yes, you were. You knew I would, John." She stepped back, looked at his clothes, and forced a smile. "Well—I do believe it's Benito Juárez himself."

Harrow shook his head. "Juárez is dead, I'm not."

"Go on, finish it. No thanks to Sue Deevers, right?"

"No. Jessica Starbuck, not Sue Deevers. I read the papers."

Jessie turned and stared at the wall. "What do you want me to say, John? How do you think I felt, knowing I might have gotten you killed? You know what that would have done to me? Do you?" She turned to face him again. "Look at me and tell me you don't know!"

Harrow walked to a table and poured himself a glass of tequila. "All right. I know what I see. I just don't understand it."

"I had to make a choice, one I didn't like. God, do you think I knew there'd be anyone like you in that camp?" She stopped and leaned against the wall. "There are some things you don't know—things it won't do any good to go into. There were other people besides Mattie behind this. They murdered my mother and my father. There's more to it, but that's a start."

Harrow's gray eyes were steady. "I can't say much to that, now can I?" He gave a bitter laugh and downed his drink. "I'll tell you something about Mattie—or whatever the hell he or *it* was. She wore me like an old pair of socks. John Fielding Harrow, who's supposed to be so goddamn smart. I was the first person she brought into this. It was me who got half those bastards to come in." Jessie showed her surprise, and Harrow went on. "I've got some friends in this town. I know how much was stacked in the bank Mattie hit." He made a face and shook his head. "And guess which one she sent *me* to?"

"John, listen—"

He waved her words aside. "That's not important now. Something else is. You and me. How much of that was real? That's something I've got to know."

"All of it," she said honestly. "You may not believe that, and I don't expect you to forgive me—that'd be asking too much. You can hate me if you want, but maybe you can see why I did what I did. Oh, Lord, I'm sorry it happened like this, John. I'm glad to see you alive. That means everything to me."

Harrow forced a smile. "Doc and me have been through

a couple of scrapes before. When things got rough, we kind of laid low in a feed store a while. Then we joined the bystanders and gawked at all the outlaws and Rangers."

"And Doc's all right?"

"Yeah, on his way back to Tombstone. Madder'n hell at me for staying here." He paused, scowled into his drink, and set it down. "It was Doc who told me not to judge you too bad. Said you likely had a reason."

"Doc's right. And I meant what I said, John, about what happened between you and me."

Harrow looked at her and held her with his eyes. "It couldn't have gone any further, though, could it?"

Jessie shook her head. "We were meant to have what we had back there. Nothing more than that, John. You know that's so."

Harrow nodded. "I'm not going to forget you."

"Or forgive me, either," she said quietly.

"That's not—" Harrow stiffened and looked away. "Yeah, I guess maybe you're right. I don't reckon I could."

She came into the circle of his arms and buried her head against his shoulder. He held her a long moment, neither of them speaking. Finally he moved away and picked up his hat, touched her cheek with his hand, and moved to the door.

"So long, Sue Deevers. You take care of yourself."

"Yes," she said, "I will, John Harrow..."

Watch for

LONE STAR AND THE GHOST PIRATES

eighteenth novel in the exciting
LONE STAR
series from Jove

coming in January!

☆ From the Creators of LONGARM ☆

The Wild West will never be the same!

LONE STAR

LONE STAR features the extraordinary and beautiful Jessica Starbuck and her loyal half-American, half-Japanese martial arts sidekick, Ki.

____	LONE STAR ON THE TREACHERY TRAIL #1	07519-1/$2.50
____	LONE STAR AND THE OPIUM RUSTLERS #2	07520-5/$2.50
____	LONE STAR AND THE BORDER BANDITS #3	07540-X/$2.50
____	LONE STAR AND THE KANSAS WOLVES #4	07419-5/$2.50
____	LONE STAR AND THE UTAH KID #5	07415-2/$2.50
____	LONE STAR AND THE LAND GRABBERS #6	07426-8/$2.50
____	LONE STAR IN THE TALL TIMBER #7	07542-6/$2.50
____	LONE STAR AND THE SHOWDOWNERS #8	07521-3/$2.50
____	LONE STAR AND THE HARDROCK PAYOFF #9	07643-0/$2.50
____	LONE STAR AND THE RENEGADE COMANCHES #10	07541-8/$2.50
____	LONE STAR ON OUTLAW MOUNTAIN #11	07526-4/$2.50
____	LONE STAR AND THE GOLD RAIDERS #12	07635-X/$2.50
____	LONE STAR AND THE DENVER MADAM #13	07112-9/$2.50
____	LONE STAR AND THE RAILROAD WAR #14	07133-1/$2.50
____	LONE STAR AND THE MEXICAN STANDOFF #15	07259-1/$2.50
____	LONE STAR AND THE BADLANDS WAR #16	07273-7/$2.50

Available at your local bookstore or return this form to:

 JOVE
Book Mailing Service
P.O. Box 690, Rockville Centre, NY 11571

Please send me the titles checked above. I enclose _____. Include 75¢ for postage and handling if one book is ordered; 25¢ per book for two or more not to exceed $1.75. California, Illinois, New York and Tennessee residents please add sales tax.

NAME_____

ADDRESS_____

CITY_____STATE/ZIP_____

(allow six weeks for delivery)   54

The hottest trio
in Western history
is riding your way
in these giant
LONGARM
adventures!

The hottest trio in Western history is riding your way in these giant LONGARM adventures!

The matchless lawman LONGARM teams up with the fabulous duo Jessie and Ki of LONE STAR fame for exciting Western tales that are not to be missed!

_____ 07386-5	LONGARM AND THE LONE STAR LEGEND	$2.95
_____ 07085-8	LONGARM AND THE LONE STAR VENGEANCE	$2.95

Available at your local bookstore or return this form to:

 JOVE
Book Mailing Service
P.O. Box 690, Rockville Centre, NY 11571

Please send me the titles checked above. I enclose _____. Include 75¢ for postage and handling if one book is ordered; 25¢ per book for two or more not to exceed $1.75. California, Illinois, New York and Tennessee residents please add sales tax.

NAME_____

ADDRESS_____

CITY_____ STATE/ZIP_____

(allow six weeks for delivery.)

64